The Cuckoo Clock

by

John Nixon

The Cuckoo Clock

by

John Nixon

Chapter One

He had to get away.

Stan Proctor ran out of the front door of his cliff-top cottage, slamming it behind him. The door latch rattled, and the door swung open again. The rain was teeming down as he ran through the meagre front garden to the car parked on the muddy path, laughingly called a drive. The sky was black with rain and he could hear the sea, whipped up by the wind, crashing onto the rocks beneath the path. If the clock had not signalled three o'clock, and he had not known it was an August afternoon, he would have guessed it was about five o'clock on a November evening. His hair was plastered to his head and his thin shirt was all but see-through with the rain. Running round to the driver's side of the car he fumbled for the keys in his pocket, and then dropped them in an ever-growing pool of brown water at his feet. He finally got into the car and shook himself, like a dog coming out of a lake. He put the key into the ignition and pulled the starter. The engine whirred, unenthusiastically, and then died. He tried again, with the same result.

Stan had always been a sucker for cars, and even more of a sucker for what seemed to be a bargain. Now he silently cursed that man in the Rose and Crown, to whom he paid £25 for what was said to be a good car at a bargain price.

'Ford Prefect. Good car, cheap to run and easy to drive. Won't let you down.'

Isn't that what he had said?

The first time he drove it Stan was unsure, and now he realised that it was nothing but a load of unreliable junk. He got out of the vehicle, and going round to the boot took out the starting handle. The rain was even heavier as he cranked the engine. Suddenly it exploded into action, and Stan hurriedly put the handle back in the boot and drove away, wheels skidding in the mud.

He had to get away.

Stan pulled past the barn at the side of the house and on to the road itself. High hedges bordered the road for about half a mile until the road dipped down towards the sea, before rising onto the top of the cliffs out towards Seatown, a bustling town enjoying the new tourist industry and day trippers that the 1950s were bringing. As he drove, the windscreen wipers struggled to clear the water, and the dark sky made visibility very poor. He thought back to the cottage. His wife spread-eagled across the living-room floor, and the blood.

He and Edna had been happy, or at least he thought so and he thought she did too, since their marriage two years ago. He worked as a bus driver and Edna had been one of his regular passengers on her way to work at the bakery shop in Seatown. She was a pretty little thing, he remembered thinking, her dark brown, almost black hair, cut in a fashionable style and a pixy-like face with a ready smile. At thirty two years old he was thirteen years older than her, and he had wondered when he asked her out, whether she would think him too old. He recalled his pleasure when she said yes, and things had moved quickly from then on, getting married only ten months later. They had been so lucky to find the cottage on the cliff. Stan had overheard his boss talking at work about a cottage that was coming up for rent shortly because both the tenants had died, and the owners were looking for new ones. It was convenient for getting to Seatown where the bakery shop was, and where Stan's bus depot was situated. It was unusual for someone in their position to have a car, but Stan was always keen on cars, and it certainly made life easier. But now this.

He had to get away.

As the road dropped down towards the sea he could see a lorry coming in the other direction. He pulled in to the side of the road to let it past, then as he went to drive off, his rear wheels skidded in the mud again. He was afraid that he might slide over the edge, but was able to control the car and straighten it up. Concentrating on that was probably why he did not see the conglomeration of mud and rocks coming down the hillside on to the road. The slide caught the side of the car and pushed it towards the edge. This time there was no escape, and the car plunged down towards the rocks. Stan just had time to think before he and the car hit the rocks below;

I have got away.

Back at the cottage the clock showed half past three.

Chapter Two

Madeleine Porter had decided that she would like to live near the sea for a change, so she was searching the Internet for estate agents on the south coast, and then checking to see if any of the properties they had on their books would be suitable. She was a fifty-seven-year old widow; her late husband, the vicar of a neighbouring parish to where she now lived, having died fairly recently. When he died Madeleine had to leave the vicarage in which they had lived for many years, and she moved in with her brother Tim Lock, who lived in Emberton, a small market town in the south Midlands. He was unmarried at the time and the arrangement had suited them both well. However, Tim, who was two years older than Madeleine, had recently married and his new wife, Fiona, was expecting their first baby. Fiona was forty-one years old, and had no children from her first marriage, so she was very thrilled with her pregnancy.

Madeleine and Fiona got on very well, but Madeleine thought that with a new baby in the house, she might be in the way. Both Tim and Fiona had pressed her to stay, so Madeleine said that she would see what was available, and then decide what to do. Madeleine had thought to herself that the best option might be if she could rent somewhere for, say, six months of the year, initially, and then reconsider. She would be able to afford to rent, with the clergy pension she had and the death-in-service payment she had received on her husband, Richard's, death, but she did not have the capital to enable her to buy a house.

The list of estate agents seemed endless, and the lists of houses and bungalows they had available were overwhelming.

'I can't do it this way. There's just too much to look at,' she said to no one in particular.

Fiona walked into the room and sat down carefully.

'Now I've left work why don't we go down for a few days and have a look round. It's so much easier to get a feel for a place if you stay there for a day or two.'

'Good idea,' replied Madeleine. 'Where shall we go?'

'Well, where do you want to go? Where would you like to live?'

Madeleine turned round and took the road atlas out of the bookcase near her chair.

'Somewhere on the coast. Out of the town preferably, but not too far.'

'Devon? Dorset? What do you think?' Fiona asked.

'Yes, somewhere there. Look, let's check out this place, Seatown.'

Madeleine googled Seatown estate agents.

'Look at that, six of them. There must be something there worth looking at.'

'Right, let's book a local B&B; there should be plenty in a seaside town.'

Madeleine did as Fiona suggested and booked three nights for the following week. She was beginning to be quite excited about her new venture. It was about an hour and a quarter's drive from Emberton, and Madeleine said that she would drive, knowing, having had five children herself, how uncomfortable it can be, six and a half months pregnant, sitting in one position in a car for any length of time.

'You don't have to move, you know,' said Fiona. 'I feel as if I am chasing you out of your home.'

'Don't be silly,' replied Madeleine, 'once the baby has arrived you'll have plenty to do, and, anyway, I think that at my age babies are nice in small doses. I shall come and visit, and you will be able to come with the little one to stay.'

The clock struck four o'clock as she spoke.

'Do you know,' said Madeleine, 'I have always fancied a cuckoo clock. My granny had one, apparently, or so my mum told me. Don't know what happened to it, though. Richard would never let me have one; he said it would drive him mad. When I am on my own I shall go out and buy myself one.'

'Better turn off the cuckoo when we come to stay,' said Tim, as he came in from the garden. 'I'm with Richard. It would drive me bonkers as well.'

'Maybe your new addition will like coming to Auntie Madeleine's because of her clock. You'll have to put up with it then.'

Tim grinned with the expectation of such visits. He was so excited by the prospect of the baby, and couldn't wait for he, or she, to arrive. They had decided not to be told the baby's sex beforehand, preferring the more old-fashioned way of the surprise.

'Have you decided what you are doing then?' he asked.

'Yes, Fiona and I are going down to Seatown on the south coast next week for three days, to do some house-hunting. It will have to be somewhere rented, but there should be plenty in and around a seaside resort. There are lots online, but I want to see them first hand. We can take it easy and have a bit of a holiday at the same time. In a few weeks Fiona is going to be thinking about things other than my housing arrangements.'

'Sounds good. Choose somewhere nice so we can come and scrounge a holiday with all the kids.'

Fiona looked up at him and smiled.

'One at a time Tim, please. Let's hope the weather stays fine so we can have a good look round. When we have chosen you can come and have a look and give it your approval.'

Chapter Three

Mary Treacy's funeral was a quiet affair. One or two of her near neighbours had gone, but no family. She had been an only child. Mary had moved to Seatown three years ago after a lifetime of living and working in France. She had had a slight stroke and decided that she would like to come back to the town where she grew up. Her work in France as a translator had given her enough money to be able to buy a small flat in the centre of town, and provide a comfortable income for her to live on.

The funeral was at the local crematorium; with the impersonal seating and detached feel so common in crematoria all over the country. The neighbours were sitting in the front two rows of chairs as the duty minister, a woman from the local Methodist chapel, started the proceedings. At that moment the side door opened and an elderly man entered, nodded his apologies to the minister, and sat in the back row.

At the end of the service the neighbours turned to acknowledge the elderly gentleman, wondering who he was, and what connection he had with Mary. He had white hair, thinning on top, and was very smartly dressed in a dark grey suit with a black tie held in place with a diamond pin. He nodded again to them as he left.

Dilys and Anne, two of Mary's neighbours followed him out, determined to speak with him, but as they left the building they saw him get into a new Jaguar and drive away.

'Who was that then?' asked Dilys, knowing her companion did not know the answer, 'and what was he doing here?'

Anne was inspecting the floral tributes left for Mary, and noticed one in particular. 'Look at this one,' she said pointing to a small bouquet of red roses. It had been delivered by a local florist, but that would not mean the giver was necessarily local.

'JTAJX. Whatever does that mean?'

'Dunno, but he was a swish-looking bloke, if it was the white haired old boy,' replied Dilys.

'Come on,' said Anne, 'I'm dying for a cuppa.'

The two women walked across the car park, each pondering who he was.

As the Jaguar drove away from the crematorium the driver smiled to himself and thought how lucky that he had seen that piece in the local paper. He could so easily have missed it, and that would have been very sad.

'I wonder if she made a will?' he mused, 'must get Hughes & Lewis to have a look.'

Hughes & Lewis were a long-established firm of solicitors in Seatown whom he had used for many years. He was sure that they would be able to discover whether Mary had made a will, and if so who the executor or executors were. It had been a very long time, but it was important to him to see it through. He thought he, and she, deserved that, at least.

Chapter Four

'Any news on The Haven?'

Matthew called across the office of Tomkins and Snell, the largest estate agents in Seatown. The office was situated in the town square and the old building they inhabited had been a feature of the town for many years. Tomkins had been selling and letting houses in Seatown and the surrounding area for more years than any of the current staff could remember. Matthew Collins was the deputy manager. He had joined the company seven years ago when he left the local college, deciding that the rat race of university entrance was not for him. He was popular with the clients, and was very successful in matching people to houses. Clive Redding, the manager, knew he was lucky to have him.

'No. Nobody. Funny, really, this time of year. You would think there would be some takers for a place like that. Mind you, the owner's a bit odd.' replied Samantha.

In Clive Redding's eyes Samantha was the direct opposite of Matthew. Where he was keen and interested, she was bored and indifferent. Her choice of clothes was controversial. Her preference for very low-cut blouses and tops, together with short skirts was not one endorsed by her colleagues, Elizabeth and Zuleika. Clive was not keen either, and together with her attitude, she was one employee he would be quite happy not to have. He did appreciate though, that dress codes were notoriously difficult to enforce, and her work performance did not, on its own, warrant dismissal.

'Might have to go back to holiday lets if he doesn't get someone soon.' Samantha continued.

The Haven was a cliff-top cottage about four miles outside the town. It had gorgeous views across the cliffs and sea, but in bad weather it was very exposed. The road from the town snaked across the cliffs, down towards the sea, and then uphill to the cottage which was perched high up. It faced the sea and had a pretty front garden and a track where it was possible to park. On the other side of the track were about fifty yards of grass before the cliff edge, and a drop of two hundred feet onto rocks.

For many years it had been rented out as a weekly holiday let, but last year the then owner decided he had had enough, and had put it up for sale. To the general surprise of the staff at Tomkins it had sold almost immediately, at the asking price, to a local businessman. Over the winter he had done some refurbishment and redecoration and he was now looking for a longer term tenant. Tomkins had suggested to him that initially he should let for six months, then he could judge whether he wanted to continue with the same tenant for a longer period. It was this six month let that was causing them difficulty.

As they were having this conversation the door opened and two women walked in; one very obviously pregnant and another, older woman who might have been her mother, but was probably not old enough. Samantha guessed, wrongly, that they were sisters.

'Good afternoon,' greeted Samantha, 'How can I help you?'

The older woman spoke first.

'Hello, my name is Madeleine Porter and this is my sister-in-law, Mrs Lock. I am looking for a house to rent temporarily. Mrs Lock is only with me today, the house will just be for me. What do you have?'

Matthew looked across the office and saw Madeleine's face as she gazed down at Samantha, who was sitting at her desk. He was not pleased with the impression which Samantha was creating. He moved across:

'Hello Mrs Porter, I'm Matthew Collins and I'm the deputy manager, I am sure we will have something that will interest you. Do come and sit down, both of you. Can I get you a drink? Tea, coffee or something cold?'

'Tea for me please,' said Fiona.

'Make that two,' added Madeleine.

'Samantha, could you get those please?'

Samantha stood up and pulled a face behind Matthew's back as she went to get the drinks. Ever likely I'm bored and you think I'm useless, if this is all I ever get to do, she thought.

'What exactly are you looking for? Do you want to buy or rent?'

Madeleine spoke:

'I'm looking to rent at the moment. Ideally I want something through the summer, say from the end of this month or the beginning of May, perhaps to October. It would be for me, but there has to be space to have people to stay, so at least two bedrooms if not three. I don't mind whether it is in the town or outside. I have a car so that's not an issue. We have looked at a couple this morning which are very promising, but we wanted to check out everything before making a decision.'

Matthew thought for a moment, wondering whether to mention The Haven, but was unsure whether its location would be suitable. He took out the details of two other houses, one in the town, part of a new development behind the shopping precinct, and a thatched cottage on the road inland.

'That looks nice,' said Fiona, pointing to the thatched offering., 'very twee. How big is it?'

'And more importantly, how much is it?' added Madeleine.

'Three bedrooms, lounge, kitchen, bathroom, downstairs cloakroom,' said Matthew.

'But how much?' persisted Madeleine.

Matthew told her and the two women winced.

'Is that the going price for all your houses? The ones we saw this morning were nowhere near that price.'

Matthew explained that the thatch made them more attractive, particularly to outsiders, and that accounted for the price. Then he decided to try it.

'There is this one,' he said, showing them the details of the cliff-top cottage. 'It's called The Haven. It used to be a holiday let but the new owner wants to rent it out for longer. It's a bit far out and it's perched on a cliff, but might be worth a look.'

Madeleine looked with interest, and at that moment Samantha returned with the tea. She leaned over provocatively towards Matthew as she put the mugs on the table. He sighed and turned away. What's the matter with him, she thought; queer? Samantha would never have said such a thing, but she could not understand why he was so disapproving of her. She saw the house information on the table and said, mischievously;

'That's on the road where that bloke got pushed off the cliff in his car all those years ago, isn't it?'

'Thank you, Samantha,' said Matthew, testily, 'That's all.'

She went and sat at the front desk, pleased with herself that she had upset him.

'What's all that about then?' asked Fiona.

Matthew realised that he would have to tell the story, or at least the story as he knew it.

'It all happened a long time ago and I only know what I do because of what my mother told me. It was back in 1954, I think, there was a terrible storm one August day. One of those when it seems like night time during the day. A young couple were living at The Haven and he left the house in the middle of the afternoon to drive into town. Sadly he never made it because there was a mudslide and rock fall along the road which crashed into the side of his car and pushed it over the cliff. They found the car in pieces on the rocks below the next day. The man's body was never found, though. The opinion at the time was that the body had been washed out to sea. Mind you they usually turn up sooner or later, don't they? Funny that.'

'Anyway the road is much better now. It has been widened over the years and a crash barrier has been put at the side of the road nearest the cliff. If you go and have a look at the cottage you'll see what I mean. If you want to know any more it was in the local paper at the time, the Haven Horror Road, the press named it. Stupid.'

Madeleine and Fiona looked at each other, intrigued and a little nervous.

'What happened to the wife?' asked Madeleine.

'Don't know. I suppose it's one of those stories where only the gory bits get remembered. Like I said, it was in the local paper at the time, or so my mum said. It was a long time ago.' replied Matthew, getting bored with the subject.

'Come on, let's have a look at the house details, never mind scaring us off with tales of old tragedies,' said Fiona, trying to get back to business.

Matthew handed over the printed details. Two bedrooms, living room, kitchen, upstairs bathroom and a small garden.

'Worth having a look at, I think,' said Madeleine. 'How much is the rent?'

'The owner is very keen to have someone in the house as soon as possible. He's been a bit mysterious, don't know why. Never looks as though he needs the money.'

The rent quoted was only slightly more than half that of the thatched cottage they had been looking at just a few moments ago.

'How do we find it? Can you give us the keys or do you have to come with us?'

Matthew looked at these two apparently respectable women and decided to take a chance. He glanced up at the clock;

'We close at six. If I give you the keys can you get them back to me before we shut? Clive, the manager, doesn't like me giving out keys to houses. I always think we're more likely to make a sale if the clients have been uninterrupted while looking around.'

'Yes, of course we can,' agreed Madeleine, 'let me give you our name and address details, and phone numbers. Then you can ring us if there's a problem and we will come back straight away. Now; directions?'

'If you're in the main car park, take the left turn at the crossroads as you come out. Take the Exeter road, then on the edge of town there is a left turn signposted to The Haven. That takes you along the cliffs, drops down to the site of the accident and then you go back uphill and the cottage is on the left. You can pull off the road and drive round to the front of the cottage. It faces the sea. The garden and the track for parking are on the sea side of the house.'

'Thanks.'

Madeleine and Fiona stood up to leave and Madeleine turning round to Samantha said;

'And thank you for the tea.'

'And for bringing up the subject of the accident. That was very interesting,' added Fiona.

Samantha smiled at them and inwardly chuckled. That'll teach him to try to hide things, she thought.

As they stood outside the shop Madeleine said;

'What's the local newspaper? I think we should look up this incident.'

'Over there,' said Fiona, pointing to a newsagents with a billboard outside.

'H'mm, *Seatown Gazette*. Probably a big day for them, the storm and the accident. Shouldn't be too difficult to find out about it.'

'Madeleine,' said Fiona, with mock sternness, 'we are here to find a house for you, not to solve sixty year-old mysteries.'

'No mystery, is there? Man falls off cliff in car during storm. That's all. Mind you, where's the body?'

'Come on, Sherlock, we have a house to view. Which way is the car park?'

Chapter Five

It was a bright, breezy afternoon as Madeleine and Fiona walked back to the car park. The two houses which they had seen in the morning were possibilities, and out of the ones they had been shown at Tomkins and Snell, the thatched one had been much too expensive and the town house was not to Madeleine's liking at all. Fiona thought that Madeleine was quite taken with The Haven, but she was uncertain. The road still sounded dangerous, and if the house was that close to the cliff any visiting children could be at risk. She was sure that Tim would be very wary about his precious offspring being so close to a cliff. It was not that Fiona would not be, but she thought Tim might be a little over-protective, bearing in mind all that had gone before.

As they got into the car Fiona said;

'What do you think, then? What is your gut feeling?'

'Like I said it sounds promising. Matthew was reluctant to mention the 'incident', I wonder why. It's years ago. Perhaps he looked at us and thought, old dear, new mother; the road will put them off.'

'We would have seen the road anyway,' said Fiona.

'Yes, but as outsiders we would not have known its history, not until it would have been too late.'

They drove out of the car park following Matthew's directions. They soon came to the sign for The Haven, and as soon as they had turned off the main road they had the most wonderful view across the cliffs and out to sea. The road ran close to the edge and they could see that the sea was perfectly still. It made it difficult to imagine a raging sea and a howling wind causing such havoc. As Matthew had said the road dropped down towards the sea and it was apparent where the road had been widened. The crash barriers on the edge were a comfort, and there was a small lay-by on the inside of the road. Madeleine pulled across and stopped.

'What a wonderful view!' she said, 'shall we get out?'

'Yes, it's quiet enough.'

They got out of the car and wandered across the road and leant on the crash barrier.

'I like it already, and I haven't seen the house yet,' said Madeleine. 'I was going to say I'll only be here during the summer months so I won't have the winter to cope with, then I remembered that storm was in August.'

'Bit of a freak, though. Should be OK, but with the weather patterns as they are you can never tell.'

'Thanks for that encouragement. I'm going to stay here and enjoy the sun and the sea, while it's pleasant.'

Fiona walked back across to the car, and sat quietly in the passenger seat. She put her hand on her tummy and visualised her, Tim and the new arrival coming to visit. If Madeleine was here for six months, or longer, they would have plenty of time. Only ten weeks to go. It was her first baby and she was so excited. The creation of a new life with the man she loved so dearly was too wonderful for her to comprehend, but she knew it was happening all the time to people all over the world. She thought back to the question Madeleine had asked at the estate agents, 'what happened to the wife?' Matthew had not mentioned children, but he had said they were a young couple. As she sat there her hand jumped as the life within her made itself known, kicking out to one side. Tears of joy formed in the corners of her eyes, and by the time Madeleine returned they were flooding down her cheeks.

'Whatever's the matter?' asked Madeleine, alarmed at the sight.

Fiona snuffled and assured her that nothing was amiss, but that she was enjoying her baby, even before the birth.

'So what did happen to the wife?' she asked Madeleine, once she had dried her tears. 'Husband goes off, has terrible accident, then she is written out of the story. Very strange. If you move in here this will be a little challenge for you. It'll keep you occupied on those dark, stormy August afternoons.'

'That's in very poor taste,' chided Madeleine, 'but you're right, it will. Of course I may not like the house. It could be about to fall into the sea, we must go and find out.'

She started the car and began to climb a steep hill back to the top of the cliffs. A short way along hedges appeared both sides of the road, which made seeing the view more difficult. As it was getting later in the day the sun was also blinding on occasions.

'Is that it?' asked Fiona as a barn came into view on the left of the road.

'I think it might be.'

Madeleine turned off the road and alongside a rather dilapidated barn. She followed the track round the barn and then they could see the house. The track was somewhat muddy, but finding a dry spot, she pulled up and stared.

'What a wonderful house, and what a tremendous view.'

The house faced the sea, as the estate agents had said, but, unusually they had underplayed its position. There was a small front garden, with some plants struggling to grow against the sea spray and the wind, and a secure fence surrounding it. As a holiday cottage it would be an essential, thought Fiona.

The front of the house was like a child's drawing; a door in the middle and a window each side of the door, and two windows upstairs, matching them. They walked round the side and there was a small window which gave into the living room. The back of the house was flat onto the road, and the other side had the barn attached. The exterior paintwork had clearly been done recently, and it looked very neat and tidy. Both women stood with their backs to the front door and gazed at the magnificent view; a clear blue sky, a cool breeze and the sun starting to set in the west.

'I can see now why it would be a great success as a holiday cottage,' said Madeleine, 'I wonder why the new owner doesn't want to continue with that?'

'Maybe he hasn't anyone to come in and check and clean every week, and doesn't fancy doing it himself. He might like the idea of having someone here he can rely on, and not take the risk every week that someone will come who will trash the place. You never know who you might get each week.'

'That's true. Right; I have the key, let's explore inside,' said Madeleine, fishing in her handbag for the key attached to a large cotton reel.

Madeleine put the key in the door and turned it, expecting some resistance, but there was none as the lock gave way without a sound. She pushed the door open tentatively and stepped inside, surprised to see a deep-pile carpet in the hallway.

'Better take our shoes off, I think.' Fiona said.

They put their shoes to one side as they closed the front door, leaving the hallway rather dark. There was a door immediately to the left which Fiona opened; it was the living room, bathed with glorious sunlight coming through both the front and side windows. There was a wood burning stove on the back wall, comfortable chairs and again, a deep pile carpet.

'This looks more than a holiday cottage, it's as if someone lives here,' said Madeleine.

'You make me feel like Goldilocks,' said Fiona, 'where's the porridge?'

The warm sun gave a comfortable glow to the room, rendering the stove and the radiator under the front window superfluous. They both sat down;

'I feel at home already,' said Madeleine.

'Why would anybody fit out a place like this and not want to live here?' asked Fiona.

'Let's have a look at the rest before we think about that,' said Madeleine.

Across the hall was a small room set out as a dining room, with a similar carpet, expensive-looking furniture and a grandfather clock in the alcove, alongside what was once an open fire. As they moved to the kitchen at the back of the house they were expecting a fully-fitted modern kitchen, with all modern appliances and equipment, and they were not disappointed. Upstairs the bedrooms and bathroom were the same. Someone had spent a lot of money fitting out this house.

'But why?' queried Madeleine, as they sat back down in the living room. 'Why spend all this money and not enjoy it yourself? And why were the agents having so much difficulty renting it out? And why were they happy for us to come out here all on our own when the place is so immaculate and we might damage it?'

'Don't know, don't know and don't know are the answers to those questions,' replied Fiona. 'But here are one or two possibilities. First question; he or she who has spent all this money is enjoying it, although we can't see how at the moment. Second question; do we know they were having difficulty? How many people have they sent out? Maybe there are snags associated with it that we are unaware of, or maybe people are put off by the high quality of the furnishings. Perhaps the owner is just choosy about who rents it.   Third question; I think we look pretty respectable and you look a likely tenant.'

'Fair enough, but the rent is ridiculous for this quality,' said Madeleine. 'There must be something else going on. I suggest we return to Tomkins and Snell and ask some more questions. There's more to this than meets the eye; and if there isn't, I shall snap his hand off.'

'Where's the place for your cuckoo clock, then? You won't be allowed to knock a nail in, you know,' teased Fiona.

They looked around the room and could find nowhere. They left the room with admiring backward glances. Putting their shoes back on they walked out to the car, which Madeleine turned round, not without some difficulty, and they returned to Seatown. The town square clock was showing half past five as they drew into the car park.

'Good timing,' said Madeleine.

On returning to the estate agents they noticed that neither Matthew nor Samantha was there. Clive Redding , the manager, came forward.

'Hello Mrs Porter, Mrs Lock. Matthew told me that he had given you the key to The Haven. What did you think?'

'We were surprised,' said Madeleine, 'clearly a lot of work has been done there, and to be honest we are surprised that it is still available.'

'Yes, I know what you mean. The owner is very particular. We have had a number of clients who wished to rent it, but the owner has not been happy. If you want to go ahead with the rental it would be necessary for you to meet him at the house. I'm sorry, but those are my strict instructions.'

'You mean he would want to vet me? I can supply you with references if you wish; my late husband was a vicar and I know that the Bishop would be very happy to provide a reference. I can also pay three months rent upfront if that is necessary.'

'Thank you, Mrs Porter, but that will not be necessary. No references will be required nor a deposit. A meeting with the owner is all that is required, but you must understand that his decision is final.'

'I understand,' said Madeleine, still a bit puzzled by this odd arrangement. 'When would he want to meet me?'

'I will have to check that with him, but it will probably be one day next week. Would that be convenient for you?'

Madeleine looked at Fiona who nodded.

'I think so, but there is one thing. Before I make a final decision would it be possible for my brother to come and have a look at the house? I do value his opinion.'

'Matthew took your details, didn't he? When are you returning to Emberton?'

'Tomorrow, but I could come back another day easily enough.'

'Leave it with me. I will ask the owner and try to arrange a date next week when you could come with your brother, and meet the owner at the same time.'

Madeleine said thank you and shook Clive's hand; it was clammy and cold. She and Fiona left the shop, her hand still damp from Clive's handshake.

'How very odd.'

Fiona agreed, but there was nothing that they could do but wait. The house was perfect, and if Madeleine could rent it for six months it would be ideal. When they were back in their hotel room Madeleine phoned Tim and told him about the house, and the strange arrangements that went with renting it. He was of the opinion that she should steer clear of unusual deals, but he could tell by her voice that she was very keen. Tim worked part-time for the local council, and spent most of his spare time on his allotment which was attaining a high reputation for organisation and appearance, not to mention produce. However he said he would be free on Thursday the following week, and hoped that would suit the mysterious landlord.

Madeleine rang off and she and Fiona went down to dinner with plenty on their minds; Matthew's story of the incident on the road, the perfect house and the pernickety landlord...and then there was the wife who never got a mention.

Chapter Six

The alarm buzzed insistently at John Williams' bedside, and an arm snaked out from under the duvet to cut the noise. He was not a stop-in-bed man, never had been. During his working life he had always aimed to be at his desk by seven-thirty, and since his retirement from his position as Chief Executive of Professional Packaging Services, or PPS as it was more commonly known, his routine in the morning had not changed. Alarm at six thirty, up, shower, dress and shave by seven, coffee followed by a brief drive into the office. The only bit that had changed of course was the drive. He continued as chairman of the board, and he was the majority shareholder. His position as chairman only took up one or two days a week, but that depended on the time of year.

He had established his company forty years ago as a small enterprise providing cardboard boxes to industry. Initially he had rented premises on the outskirts of Bridport. Over the years the business had prospered and he had expanded into production as well as supply. Now the business had a worldwide turnover of approximately sixty million pounds, making and supplying every type of packaging imaginable. He stepped down nine years ago, feeling that at the age of seventy, younger men and women were more able to face the challenges ahead. Since that time the explosion of online shopping had led to a substantial increase in business, everything needed packaging, and PPS was there to pack it, as their advertising said.

Sitting down in the kitchen of his cottage he looked across the garden to the cliffs and the sea. If only... His life was very comfortable now; a beautiful thatched cottage in a very desirable village in the county, a garden tended professionally to a high standard, apart from the bit he liked to potter in, cleaning, laundry, everything done for him. A new Jaguar in the garage. But something, or someone was lacking. John had married relatively late in life, when he was in his early forties. He had been very fond of Carole, who had been his PA for many years. When they married he was looking forward to sharing his life with someone at last. But it was not to be. Carole died three years later of breast cancer, aged only forty five. He was devastated and threw himself even more vigorously into his work. But even with Carole, much as he loved her, he knew there was something missing, something he did not think he would ever be able to regain.

His thoughts were interrupted by the ringing of the phone. Looking at the clock he saw that it was barely nine o'clock. Someone was keen.

'Hello, John Williams speaking.'

'Good morning Mr Williams, this is Hughes and Lewis, I have Mr Lewis for you. I'll put you through.'

'Good morning John, not too early for you I hope?'

He heard the familiar voice of the senior partner Jeremiah Lewis. It had been many years since there had been a Mr Hughes in the firm, and Jeremiah himself, at the age of eighty-one, was only available for the more prestigious clients.

'Morning Jeremiah. What do you have for me?'

John was thinking back to the funeral of Mary Treacy which he had attended recently, and the subsequent enquiry he had made about a will.

'Mary Treacy,' said Jeremiah, in his most lawyerly voice, 'bit naughty of you asking us to find out details of her will. Confidential, you know that.'

'Yes, I do know. But there was a particular reason.'

'I don't want to know,' replied Jeremiah, 'but I can tell you something that should interest you. Mary Treacy made a will dated 19 July 2011, and we are the executors.'

'I thought you weren't supposed to tell me,' John chipped in.

'Well I can, because you are the sole beneficiary. Oddly enough, we were going through her papers the day you phoned with your enquiry, so we would have been in touch with you anyway.'

There was a sudden pause. John had difficulty in composing himself. This was not what he was expecting at all.

'Sorry, can you say that again?' he asked.

'As I said, you are the sole beneficiary. There is a small flat in the town, a little bit in the bank, an ISA and a few shares. Not a fortune, but not too bad. Do you mind my asking; who was she?'

John steadied himself.

'I can't tell you. One day maybe, but not now. What do I need to do? Anything? Presumably you will deal with everything and let me know in due course?'

'Yes, that's right. It will probably be a few months before it's all sorted, but I can't see any major problems. I'll be in touch, or to be more accurate our probate department will be. Glad to be the bearer of glad tidings. Bye John.'

Jeremiah rang off, leaving John still holding the phone his end, staring into space. He tried to collect his thoughts and understand what it was all about.,

It would have to wait for now, because he had to prepare for the other business of the day, which had been arranged after an enthusiastic phone call last week, and that had to be handled very carefully indeed.

Chapter Seven

Madeleine and Fiona had enjoyed the rest of their stay on the south coast. The weather had held and after breakfast the following day, having checked out of the hotel, they decided to have a drive around, to take in the surrounding countryside. Madeleine was very excited about her potential new home, and wanted to go back to have another look. Although Fiona was wary, they drove along the cliff road past the house, but did not stop. On their way home Madeleine pronounced the trip a success, clearly indicating that she was going to move, even if The Haven was not possible.

Tim was very impressed with what they told him about the house, and while he was cautious, he could see that both his sister and his wife were very much in favour of the idea. He just hoped it would not end in disaster, or that they would end up being disappointed.

A couple of days later, on the Saturday following their visit, Madeleine received a telephone call from Tomkins and Snell;

'Hello, Mrs Porter, this is Clive Redding from Tomkins in Seatown. We spoke last week about the possibility of you renting The Haven. I have spoken to the owner who tells me that he is seeing someone on Tuesday next week, but he would be happy to see you on Thursday if the Tuesday interview does not prove satisfactory. I'm sorry, but he hadn't told me about the Tuesday one. I think he must have arranged it himself. He has promised to let me know as soon as possible so that I can keep you in the picture. If you find something else in the meantime I will understand completely.'

Madeleine sighed.

'I must say I had set my heart on it. It's very disappointing to hear that someone else may get in first. I am not going to look elsewhere until I know that this is resolved. Thank you for phoning.'

'I will let you know as soon as I can,' Redding assured Madeleine. 'It's very frustrating for us too. I will be in touch. Goodbye.'

Madeleine conveyed the bad news to Fiona and Tim. The fact that they were downcast about it made all of them realise how much they wanted it. A nervous weekend was endured by all as they waited and hoped, unkindly, which they acknowledged to their shame, that the Tuesday interview would not work out satisfactorily.

Tim worked for the first three days of the week, so he was not at home on Tuesday when the expected call was due. Madeleine and Fiona both stayed in so as to not miss the call. Each time the phone rang, they jumped up to answer it, and each time they were disappointed. Tim arrived home at half past five and was expecting to hear some news, but there was none. Just before six o'clock the phone rang again. Madeleine picked it up, and her face lit up, no words were necessary. She put the phone down and said;

'It's on for Thursday.'

'Hold on,' said Tim, 'we've been told that he will see us on Thursday. No more.'

Tim's caution was ignored as both women exchanged happy smiles.

'What time?' asked Fiona.

'Three o'clock. At the house, Clive Redding said he would not be there, but the owner will meet us there so we will not need a key.'

'Plenty of time to get there, then,' said Tim, being practical.

Thursday couldn't come quickly enough. It was as if they were going on a major expedition, not just to view a house.

The weather was fine and warm again, which was fortunate as Madeleine wanted Tim to see the house at its best. She had explained to him the quality of the furnishings and the appearance and situation of the cottage, so he had high expectations. They drove down to Seatown, through the town and along the now familiar cliff road, then down and up again to the house. The barn appeared on the left-hand side of the road and Tim swung the car in and round to the other side of the house. There, parked outside, was a gleaming, brand-new Jaguar.

'That didn't come cheap,' said Tim, 'that model £60,000 plus, I should think.'

He parked his more modest six-year old Volvo in front of it, and as he did so he saw a figure by the living room window. As they got out of the car the front door opened, and a smartly dressed man, probably in his late seventies, spoke;

'Good afternoon. I'm John Williams, and you must be Mrs Porter,' he said addressing Madeleine.

'Hello Mr Williams, do call me Madeleine, it sounds so formal otherwise. This is my brother Tim and his wife Fiona. Fiona and I visited the house the other day. We were very taken with it.'

'Thank you Madeleine, do call me John.'

Introductions over, John Williams invited them into the living room, where he had prepared afternoon tea for them. As they walked in Madeleine gave a gasp of astonishment.

'That wasn't there the other day. It's wonderful.'

She pointed to the wall with the wood burner set in it. Above the mantelpiece was the most magnificent cuckoo clock.

'Madeleine,' said John, 'I am pleased to say I am delighted to rent the house to you.'

'But we've hardly met, you know nothing about us,' said Tim.

'Tim, I know all I need to know about your sister from her reaction to the clock. It is my most treasured possession, and this house has been furnished around it. I know that sounds odd. I can't have it at home, because it belongs here. And it needs someone who will cherish it as I do. And that someone is your sister.'

He changed the subject immediately.

'Come on, do sit down, Milk, sugar?'

They settled down in the comfortable chairs and enjoyed the tea and cakes that John had prepared. During the conversation that followed, which was on trivial subjects, Madeleine kept looking up at the clock. What had been there when she and Fiona came to see the house earlier? They had said about space to put a clock, and there wasn't any. They would have noticed that clock, of course. Then she remembered; a nondescript print of The Needles off the Isle of Wight was hanging above the wood burner. But the real question remained, what was it doing here now, and why was it his favourite possession? And if that were the case why not have it at home? She could contain herself no longer, she would have to ask:

'I love the clock, and I am sure if it were mine I would want it at home.'

She did not feel she could ask him outright why it was here.

'This is its home. I can't explain any more.' John replied. 'If you are going to rent the house, then it has to be here.'

'Yes, of course. That's no problem,' replied Madeleine, not wishing to antagonise him.

'Let me show you all the rest of the house. I know you two ladies have seen some of it before, but I would like to show it to you again.'

John led them through the downstairs, then upstairs, showing them all the rooms, cupboards, heating system and plumbing. Then he took them outside, round to the barn and into the garden and over to the cliff.

'All the land between the road and the cliff belongs to the house,' he explained, 'but the garden is fenced to provide an element of safety, but care still needs to be taken, especially with children,' he added looking at Fiona.

'Thank you for taking such trouble,' said Tim, 'the house is delightful.'

'And the position, with the wonderful sea views,' added Fiona.

As she said this there was a fleeting look that crossed John's face, so briefly that it was almost indistinguishable, but Madeleine had noticed it.

'I will ring Clive Redding at Tomkins,' said John, returning to business. 'He will arrange the necessary paperwork. When would you like to move in, Madeleine?'

'First week in May? What's the date after the Bank Holiday?'

'Bank Holiday is the 6th,' said Tim.

'The 7th it is then,' said Madeleine.

'Yes, that will be fine,' replied John. 'I'll tell Tomkins.'

They shook hands and returned to Tim's car. He reversed gingerly out along the track and turned into the road. There was a thoughtful silence as they drove away, each of them pondering in their own way what the history of this treasured clock was.

Chapter Eight

Tina Jenkins was thin. She knew she was thin, and she didn't like it. She also knew that these days you were meant to look like that, because that's what the models in the magazines looked like. But she didn't want to be thin. She wanted hips and breasts that would give her the curves she so desired. To try to achieve this she ate a lot, but she didn't put on the weight she craved, much to her disappointment, although Kevin, her partner, did not seem to mind at all.

They lived in the part of Seatown not on the tourist trail, in a street of 1950s built council houses, now surrounded by 1980s built flats and maisonettes. She had lived here since she married Brian in 1989, and she had her only child, James, or Jimmy as she always called him, later the same year. Tina Hawkes she was then; new wife, new mum. She was happy. But it didn't last very long. Soon after Jimmy was born, Tina discovered that Brian's affections were spread far and wide, and then, when little Jimmy was six, he left for good.

At least by this time Jimmy was at school, so that it was a little easier to fit in her work on the checkout at Asda. However she still needed help with childcare after school, and there was none available from parents on either side. She struggled on with help from voluntary organisations and church groups, and then in 2007 she met Kevin Jenkins, a thirty-two year old youth worker. Tina had divorced Brian in 2001 but she was in no hurry to remarry. However, she did love Kevin and he was good to her. He moved into her house in Queens Drive shortly after they met, and she was, by now, calling herself Jenkins.

Jimmy had joined the Navy in 2006 when he was seventeen and he kept in touch with his mum by phone and email from the different parts of the globe where he was stationed. He had met Kevin on a number of occasions and the two men got on well together.

Tina was standing at the kitchen sink, looking across her back garden of scrubby grass and lonely flowers; peeling potatoes and silently giving thanks for Kevin, whom she felt had rescued her from a life of misery, and Jimmy, who was as good a son as any mother could wish for. Her mobile phone, lying on the kitchen table behind her, beeped into action. Picking it up, she heard a familiar voice;

'Hello Tina, it's Brenda at the Laurels.'

Brenda was the sister at the nursing home where Tina's father lived.

'It's Dad again. I'm sorry, but it's not looking good. Can you come?'

'Kevin's out at the moment, and I don't expect him back till late this evening. Is it really bad?'

'I'm afraid so. The doctor has been this afternoon, and he was very pessimistic. Is there a bus?'

'No, not all the way to you. I could ask Clare to give me a lift, but she's got the children to pick up. I'll get the bus into town and then I'll have to walk. It'll be best part of an hour before I get to you.'

'I hope that will be OK. I'll see you later.'

Brenda rang off and Tina wondered. She had had phone calls like this before, and when she had dropped everything to go, it had been a false alarm. She knew that sounded harsh, but her father, Eric, was in his nineties and hadn't had a meaningful conversation with anyone for close on two years. He was looked after well enough, she accepted, but she realised it was just a matter of time really. Better make the effort, she thought, you never know. She texted Kevin to tell him what was going on, and said she was going on the bus. She was pleased to receive a reply almost immediately saying that he would come home and take her. That made her feel warm inside.

Kevin arrived home twenty minutes later and Tina was ready and waiting.

'Come on, love, get in,' he said.

They drove through the estate and across town to the large house in a leafy avenue off the Dorchester road. It was the type of house built originally for professional men and their families, and probably a couple of maids. Doctors, lawyers, headmasters and local captains of industry would have once owned these houses. Now they were almost exclusively dental surgeries, solicitors' offices, or residential and nursing homes.

As Kevin turned into the drive they saw Brenda waiting at the front door. Tina had phoned to say that Kevin was bringing her, and Brenda had been pleased because it seemed time was of the essence. As they got out of the car she steeled herself to give them the bad news. She went over to them and hugged Tina;

'I'm sorry,' she said, 'your dad died a few minutes ago. It was all very peaceful. I think he had just had enough,'

Tina sobbed into Brenda's shoulder. Breaking away from her she tried to dry her eyes, but the tears kept coming. Brenda handed her a box of tissues and she tried again. Her relationship with her father had always been a tricky one. He was quite an old father, nearly fifty when she had been born, and she never felt that he and her mother, who was much younger, were a very good match. After Tina had married Brian and had Jimmy, she did not see much of her mum and dad. By this time her dad was in his seventies and her mum only in her early fifties. The marriage did not last much longer, the divorce finally coming through in 1993, and Tina had seen nothing of her mother from that day to this. Her father could be argumentative and had a temper, and as he aged that became worse. Tina had persuaded him to go into a residential home, and then after the dementia had set in he was moved to the nursing side of the home. That was when she had first met Brenda.

'Can I see him?' she asked.

'In a minute,' replied Brenda,' come in and sit down and I will get you a cup of tea. Then when we have tidied him up you can see him.'

Brenda guided Tina and Kevin into the waiting area and went to make the drinks.

'He could be an awkward old so-and-so,' she said, 'and he had a terrible temper. I remember when I was a little girl my mum said something, and he raged at her and didn't speak to her for days. I have no idea what that was about, but I remember it as clearly as if it were yesterday.'

'I never met him properly,' said Kevin, 'what did he do? What did he like?'

'He was a mixture. Like I said he had this temper which would rage up from nowhere, but he was good to my mum, and she didn't appreciate him. He was a great cricket fan in later life. He was always in work, different things, nothing posh, but he was a hard worker and faithful to her. He didn't deserve how she treated him.'

Brenda returned with the tea.

'Drink that and then I'll see whether you can go in,' she said.

Kevin and Tina sat in silence, looking around at the garish walls, wondering how many other families had sat here, and how many more would, waiting to take last leave of their loved ones. It was a depressing thought that it all ended like this. Tina was not a woman of any faith, and so for her the end was the end, and that made it more difficult.

There was a knock on the door, and a nurse entered and spoke to Brenda.

'You can come through now,' Brenda said to Tina and Kevin, 'would you like me to come with you?'

'Yes, thank you,' replied Tina, thankful for Brenda's help.

Tina and Kevin walked through into the room where Eric Smith was lying. He had been a powerful man, short, but with broad shoulders. Now he looked shrivelled. His strong arms that used to carry her up to bed were no more, his bright beaming face that kissed her goodnight now in sad repose Tina tried to tell herself that he had been in his nineties and that was a 'good innings', but when it came to it no age was good enough. She burst into tears and cried out:

'Dad,' as she bent down and kissed him on his forehead for the last time.

Chapter Nine

As they arrived back in Emberton Fiona suggested that they should pick up an Indian takeaway so that they did not have the trouble of preparing a meal after a long day. The suggestion was greeted with enthusiasm all round. Tim parked behind the restaurant and they walked round to the front and perused the menu in the window. It was unnecessary as Tim and Madeleine always had the same, and Fiona was happy with any of the vegetarian options. They went inside and ordered, and were told it would be twenty minutes. Tim offered to take the two women home and then come back to pick up the meal, which was readily agreed to.

Madeleine and Fiona welcomed the opportunity to chew over the day's events without Tim being present. They felt sometimes that they could not give voice to their more outlandish theories when he was around. He was much too practical. Settled in the comfort of their own home they began to consider what would prompt a man to furnish a house so elegantly and tastefully to house a clock.

'It's nonsense,' said Madeleine, 'nobody is going to do that for a clock. Nobody is going to spend thousands of pounds, because that's what he must have spent, without some ulterior motive.'

'That's very harsh,' replied Fiona, 'what motive could he possibly have? He told us why he had done it. Why do you not believe him?'

'It's not that I don't believe him, I just think there is more to it.'

'More to what? Here's a man with a lot of money to hand, nothing and no one to spend it on, so he buys and furnishes a house in which to keep a memento. Maybe nuts, but then...'

Madeleine sat, puzzled. She was unable to formulate her ideas, but she was confident that in the background there was something, some tiny fragment, which would unlock the mystery.

They heard the car return and Tim came in with a carrier bag full of sweet-smelling goodies. They had not had much to eat today, and they set about the meal with gusto.

'What's the answer, then?' said Tim, as he wiped up the sauce from his plate with the last piece of naan bread. 'I'm sure you will have it all worked out by now. How long was I gone? Twenty minutes, plenty of time.'

'If only,' said Madeleine. 'We are not even agreed that there is a mystery. Fiona thinks that what he told us is the truth, the whole truth and nothing but the truth.'

'I wouldn't go that far,' objected Fiona. 'I said that he had told us why he had done what he had, and that I thought it was reasonable.'

'It is a bit odd, though,' said Tim. 'Madeleine, when you have got yourself sorted out Fiona and I are expecting you to find out all about it and report back. The baby is due in nine weeks, so that doesn't give you much time.'

'I think I shall need more time than that, Tim. I've got to move house first, and then find my way around everywhere. You know how these things can drag on.'

Tim thought back to their own experiences of tracing the past, both personally and involving other people. She was right; it did take time, always more than expected.

'OK then, Christmas.'

'There will be enough time for that, but first I need to start thinking about moving out. May is only a couple of weeks away. I shall not need to take furniture, clearly. I don't think any of ours could match what's there anyway. The kitchen was very well-equipped and there was bedding and everything. It'll be more like going on a long holiday; I'll just need clothes and personal bits and pieces.'

'And laptop, don't forget, you can't trace the story and the history without that; well you could but it would be a lot more difficult,' added Fiona.

'Was there internet access there?' asked Tim.

'I don't know but I would be very surprised if there wasn't. It's got everything else. I'll check with Clive Redding when he's next in touch. If so there would be a phone; was there a mobile signal?'

'Check with Redding again,' suggested Tim.

Madeleine settled down for the evening, planning her move and what she would need to take. She also started to give some thought to solving the question of the clock. Early days yet, she would need to move in and familiarise herself with the area first, but she was already having some ideas.

Meanwhile Tim and Fiona's evening was more concentrated on their impending arrival. 'The bump' was very active this evening, and they were enjoying themselves feeling it move around. When Fiona first told Tim she was pregnant he had rushed out to buy lots of baby things. Fortunately Fiona had been able to sift through his purchases and return those which were unnecessary. Since then they had done the baby shopping together, Tim realising that his knowledge of such things was very limited.

Fiona's adopted daughters, Victoria and Grace, had been very thrilled with the news of Fiona's pregnancy, and though they were away at university they kept up with her progress by text and email. She was also pleased that they were able to make occasional visits. They were fascinated to hear of Madeleine's proposed move to the south coast, and were intrigued by the story of the clock. It was becoming a family affair, and Madeleine had been instructed to solve it as soon as possible. However she knew from previous experience that it can be difficult to find answers to such questions, and sometimes the answers may not be what you would hope them to be.

The following week the paperwork arrived from Tomkins and Snell for Madeleine to complete with regard to the rental of The Haven. It was all very straightforward and there seemed no need to consult a solicitor. It was a standard six month Protected Shorthold Tenancy, widely used across the country. It was only when she saw the rental figure that she thought a mistake had been made, so she telephoned Tomkins immediately.

'Good morning, Tomkins and Snell, can I help you?'

It was Samantha who answered the phone and Madeleine recognised her voice.

'Hello Samantha, this is Madeleine Porter. Is Mr Redding available please?'

'Hello Mrs Porter. Did you like the house? It's wonderful isn't it? I'm so glad you are going to live there.'

Madeleine wondered why she was so pleased but put it down to business enthusiasm, but that wasn't the impression she had had of Samantha before.

'Yes, I did. Thank you. Is Mr Redding there?'

'Oh yes, I'll get him for you.'

She heard Samantha call across the office.

'Clive, it's Mrs Porter.'

'Thank you Samantha. I'll take it here.'

'Good morning Mrs Porter. Is everything alright? I believe it all went very well with Mr Williams last week?'

'Yes, it did, thank you. I have received in the post today the rental documentation, and I don't understand the rental figure quoted. I know when we spoke before you explained that the owner was keen to have someone, how shall I put it, special, to live in the house. But this rental of £50 per month can't be right. Shouldn't it be £500?'

'No, that is absolutely correct. Mr Williams was most emphatic. The rental is to be £50 for the first six months, and then will be subject to review in the usual way.'

'That is very generous,' said Madeleine.

'From what Mr Williams told me he was delighted to have you as a tenant. I got the impression he would have let you have it rent-free, but I suggested to him that a small rental would be better for all concerned. You would not feel so obliged, and he would get some money. The responsibility for all the bills, gas, electricity, council tax and everything is yours of course.'

'Yes, I understand that. There are a couple of other things. Is there internet access at the house? And is there a mobile signal?'

'There is a phone line but you will have to make your own arrangements about internet access. There is a mobile signal on all the major networks.'

'Thank you,' said Madeleine, 'I don't think there is anything else. I will sign these papers today and get them back to you as soon as possible. Is May 7th still OK for moving in?'

'Yes, that will be fine. When we have received the paperwork back from you and Mr Williams we will let you have your copies, and confirm the moving-in date. Is there anything else?'

Madeleine wanted to ask him what was going on with the clock but decided he wouldn't know and it would have been impertinent to ask anyway, so she kept quiet.

'No that's all. Thank you very much again.'

'Thank you Mrs Porter. Goodbye.'

During the whole of this conversation Madeleine was struck by how ordinary the situation was from Redding's point of view, except for the rental, but how extraordinary it was from hers. She had managed to find a gorgeous house for virtually no rent, which came with a lovely clock that she had always wanted, and in addition she had a project which would keep her occupied for most of the time she was going to be there. This sounded like great fun!

Chapter Ten

Tina and Kevin were sitting in the lobby area of the nursing home, stunned and lost for words. Eric had been ill for some time, and Tina had known that this day would come quite soon. It had not made coping with it any easier. She tried to think back to the good times that she and her dad had spent together, but it was difficult. Eric had been an old parent and as such, apart from the bedtime stories and occasional walk along the cliff, he had not been a close father. She remembered how, when she was little, her friends had spoken of their own fathers, how they had taken them out to the park, bought them ice-creams on sunny days, hugged them and held their hands in public. They had turned up at school events, concerts and sports days, and gone to parents' evenings to hear of their progress. Tina's father had done none of these things.

She acknowledged in her heart that he had provided for her and she had never wanted for anything. They were not wealthy by any means, but she had never had to go without ordinary home comforts. But she was never close to him. In his old age she had cared for him, and loved him in a strange way, despite his aloofness. However, she had always wished she could have got closer to him; to find out what really made him tick. She knew his likes and dislikes, although she could never get inside him, to understand him. Now, as she sat waiting for Brenda to return, she knew that she never would. There would be things to arrange, registering the death, fixing the funeral and also sorting out his clothes and personal possessions. It was not a task she was looking forward to at all.

Brenda came back through the door into the lobby, carrying a small box.

'I've gathered together your father's personal items,' she said, as she handed the box to Tina. 'What shall we do with his clothes?'

'What do you usually do?' asked Tina.

'It varies,' replied Brenda, 'sometimes relatives want to take away items of clothing that may have some sentimental value.'

'I don't think Dad will have had anything like that,' said Tina. 'Give them to charity or bin them. That's what I would have done, so it'll save me the trouble.'

Tina realised with horror how heartless that must have sounded.

'Oh, sorry. I didn't mean to sound uncaring. I don't think I could face going through his clothes, and I don't expect there's anything that I would want to keep.'

Brenda put her arms around Tina.

'Don't worry. I fully understand. It wasn't heartless; it was a very natural reaction. I will go through all his clothes myself and if there is anything that I think you might want to keep, I'll give you a ring and you can say yes or no.'

'Thank you, Brenda. You've been so helpful.'

'Would you and Kevin like another cup of tea? I'm sure you would. I will go and put the kettle on.'

She disappeared efficiently, leaving the two of them. Kevin squeezed her hand.

'There's a lot to do, but we don't have to rush. We'll have this cup of tea and then go home. I will go into town tomorrow and register the death. Once we've done that we can think about the funeral. What would he have wanted, do you think?'

'He was funny,' she replied, 'he hardly ever went to church, but I think he went to Sunday School as a child, because every so often he would get out his Bible and read aloud some of the stories from the Old Testament. You know; David and Goliath, Samson and Delilah, Moses, that sort of thing. David and Jonathan was a particular favourite. I am sure he would have described himself as a Christian, so we ought to recognise that.'

'I'll speak to the vicar tomorrow, sort something out.'

Brenda reappeared with the tea which she handed to them, and which they drank in silence; Tina thinking what a waste of time all this religion was, and Kevin imagining Eric declaiming in a loud voice those Old Testament stories.

Tea drunk, they thanked Brenda again, and, picking up the box, went out to the car. They collected fish and chips on their way home, and sat at the kitchen table, eating with their fingers; they always said it tasted better that way.

'We ought to have a look at this box,' Kevin said, 'find out the old boy's secrets.'

'Don't think he had any, did he?'

Tina was jolted into laughter by this suggestion. Anyone less likely than her Dad to have any secrets she could not imagine. Clearing away the fish and chip papers Kevin put the box on the table in the kitchen.

'Let's see,' said Kevin.

'Isn't it sad that all your life ends up in one small cardboard box?'

Kevin opened the box and started taking the contents out. He lifted out folders, receipts and small boxes.

'What's this?' he said.

'Receipts and paperwork from the home, by the looks of it,' said Tina. 'Council tax, old tax returns. Nothing very exciting.'

Kevin picked up a tattered receipt.

'This one looks interesting. Lawrence and James, High Street, Seatown, dated 23 May 1952. Nineteen shillings and eleven pence. Wonder why he kept this? What do you reckon it was for?' asked Kevin.

'Doesn't it say?' asked Tina.

'Unfortunately no, the paper's torn and you can't read that bit. Who were Lawrence and James? I don't recognise the name of the shop.'

'Can't think that Dad had anything that he would want to keep the receipt for. Nineteen shillings and eleven pence. That would've been quite a lot in 1952, wouldn't it?'

'Don't know how much, but I would think so. We'll have to make some enquiries, see what sort of shop it was. What else have you got there?' asked Kevin.

Tina took out another folder.

'Let's see, what's in here.'

Opening the folder she found correspondence from the MCC, and tickets for cricket matches that he had been to over the years. Tickets for the Benson and Hedges Final 1985, Lords Test 1973, and letters about MCC membership.

'He loved his cricket, would go whenever he could get time off work. Then there were the weekend matches as well.'

'Nothing else special here is there?'

'No. Doesn't look like it,' agreed Tina.

She lifted the box off the table and as she did so the bottom of the box gave way, and a small envelope fell to the floor.

'What was that?' asked Kevin.

'Don't know.'

She leant down and picked up the contents of the envelope, which had spilled on to the floor. She gazed at it, puzzled.

'What in heaven's name?'

'Maybe he did have a secret after all,' said Kevin.

Chapter Eleven

The day of Madeleine's move was bright and sunny, for which she was very grateful. She had moved house in the rain often enough in the past to know what that was like; wet footprints through the house, rain-soaked belongings stacked in soggy cardboard boxes, coupled with a depressing air of gloom surrounding the whole enterprise. As she hadn't needed to bring furniture and equipment she had been able to do everything herself, with the assistance of Tim and Fiona. Once all was safely unloaded they sat in the living room and, with welcome cups of tea on the table, they were able to relax and enjoy their surroundings. Tim looked up at the cuckoo clock which cuckooed the hour, four o'clock.

'That's your next assignment,' said Tim, pointing to the clock. 'Find out what is so precious about that timepiece. No one spends a fortune buying a house and furnishing it in some style, just to house a clock.'

'I have had some ideas on that,' replied Madeleine. 'I shall keep you informed. But before I get involved with that I need to settle in.'

'We shall look forward to your reports,' said Fiona, as her hand, which was resting on her lap, jerked with the movement below it.

'All of us,' she said laughing.

Before leaving for Emberton, Tim and Fiona had another look around the house, exploring the rooms more thoroughly than they had been able to previously when John Williams was there. On the landing there was a hatch for the loft.

'Have you been up here?' asked Tim.

'No, I wasn't sure if I should.'

'Well you're renting the whole house, why not? Have you got a ladder or a stepladder?'

Tim reached up to the hatch, and when he moved it he was surprised when a built-in ladder dropped down to the floor.

'Let's explore,' he said, enthusiastically.

'I think I'll stay down here,' said Fiona. 'I don't want to get stuck halfway.'

'Good idea,' said Madeleine. 'Go on Tim, you go and have a look for us.'

Tim climbed the stairs gingerly, and peered through into the darkness. He felt the wall inside and found a light switch. Turning it on he could see the room was full of odd bits of furniture, stacked haphazardly against the walls.

'Looks as if this is what he did with the old furniture,' he called down. 'Only good for firewood, as far as I can see.'

He stepped into the room to examine the contents more closely. There were old dining chairs with broken struts, a couple of armchairs with worn armrests and cushions and a tallboy piled high with dog-eared books, a table lamp and an ashtray. A rusty iron bedstead stood on its end against one of the walls.

'There's a lot of stuff up here,' he called, 'don't know how he got it all up here,' he paused, 'hold on, there's a door at the other end, I'll go and have a look.'

Tim clambered across the joists, careful not to knock over the piles of junk. Reaching the far side of the attic he opened the door, which he expected to stick and squeak, but it did neither. As he opened the door he saw a staircase leading downwards, and realised that what he was looking at was the inside of the barn which adjoined the house. The larger items had clearly been brought up to the attic through the barn, but he was puzzled why anyone would want to keep this old furniture, when the house was so beautifully furnished with new. He closed the door and made his way back across the attic to the hatch, where Madeleine and Fiona were waiting for his report.

'Most of it seems to have been taken up through the barn; there's a staircase that runs down from the loft. But why? That's what I can't fathom.'

'Something else for Madeleine to find out, then,' said Fiona. 'You're going to be very busy,' she added, turning to her sister-in-law.

'I want to have a look in the barn before we go,' said Tim.

Tim led them out of the front door and round into the dilapidated structure attached to one side of the house. Inside they found more bits and pieces of household equipment, an antiquated Hoover vacuum cleaner, a stained flat iron and scratched saucepans, along with rusty tools and long-unused gardening equipment. Also pushed against one of the side walls was a four-square table, of the kind Tim remembered having seen in old films set during the War. The table was ringed and stained from years of use and had a deep gouge across one corner. On the table was a battered cardboard box with a faded address written on it. The contents of both the barn and the loft were in stark contrast to the rest of the house, as if there had been an attempt to preserve something of the old house, while making it new.

As they went back to the house the cuckoo reminded them of the time, and Tim and Fiona said their goodbyes. They were looking forward to their return after the baby was born, and waved as they set off along the cliff road to Seatown. The sun was still shining as Madeleine poured another cup of tea and sat in the small front garden, admiring the view from her house, thinking how lucky she had been. She had never had a house of her own; the many vicarages she had lived in during her married life had always felt temporary, and while she had enjoyed living with Tim, it was his house, not hers. She knew that this was only for six months initially, but it felt like hers and not someone else's. Also, you never knew what might be round the corner. She was looking forward to a new and exciting phase in her life, as she gently nodded off in the late afternoon sun.

Chapter Twelve

Despite what she had said to Tim and Fiona, Madeleine was very keen to get started on her investigation into the clock business. She recalled what the estate agent had said about the 'Haven Horror Road' incident, and while she could not see a direct connection between that and the clock, she felt it was something relating to the house, and therefore might be a useful place to begin. She needed to go into Seatown to buy some food and she wanted to have a look round the town to see what other shops there were. As a regular churchgoer she also wanted to have a look inside the town church, and check out the times of services.

Seatown was a typical seaside holiday town; bright and colourful in the summer, dark and gloomy during the winter months. There was a large market square which was peopled by stalls of many different colours, selling everything you could want; food, clothing, buckets and spades, leather goods and all manner of household and kitchen equipment. Parking in the main car park she wandered through the stalls without buying anything but enjoying the energy and enthusiasm of the stallholders as they peddled their wares. On the edge of the market square were other shops; a baker's, a greengrocer's, an electrical shop as well as a large Co-operative department store. The market bustled with people, holidaymakers and townsfolk alike. Madeleine remembered a friend of hers who had lived in a seaside resort telling her that you could tell who the locals were because they wore suits and walked in the gutter. Madeleine had been puzzled by this, until the friend explained that with crowded pavements the quickest way to get around the town was to walk in the gutter, and no one on holiday wore a suit. As she stood in the square at Seatown, Madeleine understood perfectly.

Towards the end of the square was the imposing edifice of St Martin's Church, a solid building with a thin steeple piercing the skyline. She made her way through the throng and walked through the iron gates separating the noise and bustle of the market place from the quiet and solitude of the graveyard. A large, well-kept notice board at the entrance announced Holy Communion services at 8.00am and 10.30am each Sunday, together with other services on other days. There was also information about the local clergy and church organizations.

In the churchyard an elderly man was sitting on one of the flat gravestones. He had a trilby hat pulled down across his face, with an old raincoat around him, in direct contradiction to the pleasant spring weather. Madeleine noticed that he took a notebook from the pocket of his raincoat and scribbled something down as he gazed across the market place. She was standing about thirty yards away from him, so she did not think that he had seen her; indeed he appeared to be oblivious to everything that was going on around him. She knew from her experience of living next door to churches, that different people used the churchyard in their own different ways. For some it was somewhere to sit down and rest, for others somewhere to contemplate the loss of a loved one, and others an opportunity to think about life in general. She turned away from watching the old man to look at the notice board.

As she stood reading the board a man was walking down the path from the church;

'Hello, can I help you?' He said pleasantly.

'Hello,' replied Madeleine, 'I'm new to the area and I was just checking on the service times. Are you the vicar?'

'No.' The man chuckled. 'Not me, I'm only one of the stewards here. I'm Ian, Ian Clay. We like to try to keep the church open during the day, but we've found that it's too risky to have it open without someone being around. Sad really, that you can't trust people not to steal from a church. So we are open most days and we have a rota of helpers.'

'I know the problems,' replied Madeleine, 'my late husband was a vicar, and we always liked to keep the church open when we could, but it was difficult to get enough volunteers to man it. I'm Madeleine, by the way. I've moved from Emberton where I have been living with my brother. I'm now living at The Haven, do you know it?'

'Yes, the Haven Horror Road. Sorry, I shouldn't have said that. Have you heard the story? I do a bit of local history and that is probably the most exciting thing that has ever happened here.'

'Yes, the estate agent told me about it, or at least, what he knew from his mother. I am going to do a bit of digging to find out more when I have the chance.'

'If I can help, let me know. Where do you propose to start?'

'Not sure at the moment,' she said, although in her own mind she had decided to start with the local newspaper reports.

'If you need any help, let me know, I'm always willing to help a fellow historian.'

'Thank you very much,' said Madeleine, 'maybe I'll see you in church on Sunday and we could have a chat afterwards.'

'Good idea. I'm in the choir, so you won't see me beforehand, but do stay for coffee afterwards and we can talk then.'

Madeleine walked away. Nice chap, she thought. He could be useful in my inquiries.

Ian walked back to the church. She seemed friendly, he thought; wonder if she would like to join the choir. And I would love to see the inside of The Haven. He had heard that it had been done up and was now very posh.

Ian Clay was sixty four, and had been a widower for three years. His wife had been in a wheelchair for a very long time, and they had been unable to have any children. After leaving the Royal Navy he had worked at PPS for nearly twenty years, and had taken early retirement as soon as he could. Janice had been paralysed from the waist down in a riding accident when she was twenty four; they had only been married for six months. In the latter part of her life he had become her main carer as her condition had deteriorated. Neither of them had wanted her to go into a home, and when he retired he was able to devote all his time to her. He had realised, as she did, that it was not going to be for long, and she had died peacefully at home, with Ian by her side.

After having a bite to eat in a local cafe Madeleine set out to find the library, hoping they might have old copies of the local newspaper. She found it in a narrow back street, which led down to the car park. Antique shops and a second-hand bookshop jostled for space with the library, the entrance to which was not very obvious. However, once inside, Madeleine was surprised at the amount of space there was. Reminds me of Dr Who's TARDIS, she thought. A spiky-haired young man on reception showed Madeleine the Reading Room where the newspapers were available. She asked for August 1954.

'Haven Horror?' he asked. 'I know the one. Here you are.'

He handed Madeleine a large book in which were bound old newspaper copies. Putting it on the desk he opened the page.

'The *Gazette* in those days was published every Friday, so the one you want is 27 August.'

The young man left Madeleine to it. She gazed at the front page and saw the now-familiar headline:

Haven Horror Road

A man was believed killed on Tuesday afternoon this week when his car was pushed off the road by a landslide on the cliff road out of Seatown. The road runs along the top of the cliff and then dips down towards the sea before rising up the hill to the house called The Haven. It is believed that Stan Proctor, a bus driver, who lived at The Haven with his wife Edna, was driving away from his house on Tuesday afternoon when the heavy rain during the storm that day created a landslip which knocked the car across the road and over the cliff. Mr Proctor's car, a Ford Prefect, was found the following day, crushed at the bottom of the cliff. There was no sign of Mr Proctor, but it is believed that his body will have been washed out to sea. Mrs Proctor, who was not in the car, was too distressed to talk to our reporter.

Madeleine was disappointed. This report did not tell her anything more about the incident than she already knew, apart from the names of the couple involved. She turned the pages of the book and found the next two week's editions. She looked through and could find nothing. No report of a body being found, no report of how the wife was faring, it seemed very odd for a local newspaper not to follow up on a big local story. Then, four weeks later, in the edition of 24 September, she found a small piece on an inside page;

Haven Horror Road Tragedy

The body of Stan Proctor, believed to have been killed in a tragic accident on 24 August when his car was pushed off a cliff in a storm, has still not been found. Police say they would have expected it to have been washed up by now if it had gone into the sea, but there have been no reports from the coastguard to that effect. There was no comment from Mrs Proctor when our reporter spoke to her.

Madeleine asked if she could have copies of each of these reports and the assistant did that for her. She tucked them into her bag and walked back to the car park, lost in thought. This story seemed to have entered local folklore but without any satisfactory conclusion. Maybe she would enlist Ian's help after all. She was putting the key into her car door when a voice called;

'Madeleine.'

It was Ian.

'I'm off home after my stint. Have you done anything yet?'

'Hello Ian, yes, I've been to the library to look at the newspaper reports. Not very useful I'm afraid.'

'No, they're not,' agreed Ian, 'What I don't get is why nothing more was done. Didn't the wife want to know what happened?'

'You would think so, but who knows? This needs more thought. I'll see you Sunday when I have had chance to mull over these reports.'

Madeleine said goodbye and opened the door of her car. As she was driving back along the road to the house, she considered what had been said in the newspapers. Rain had started to fall as she parked outside the house.

Thinking again about the landslip, she was happy to be home.

Chapter Thirteen

John Williams was very pleased to have found a tenant for The Haven. It had taken some time, and one or two of the interviews had been difficult, especially when he had told them they were unsuitable. He had been determined to make the right choice because the clock had a very particular significance for him.

He was enjoying a morning coffee when the phone rang; it was his solicitor, Jeremiah Lewis;

'Morning John. One or two things have cropped up with regard to Mary Treacy. Can you come in today for a few minutes?'

'Er. Yes, I think so. What time?'

'Whenever you want to, but about half two this afternoon would suit me best.'

'I shall see you then.'

John was intrigued. What could Jeremiah want to see him about? The Mary Treacy will had seemed very straightforward, so he couldn't imagine what the problem might be. He had other things to do before then, but his mind was distracted by the phone call. He was very puzzled.

'Come in John,' called the solicitor. 'I wanted to talk to you about Miss Treacy.'

'Why? What's the problem?'

'No problem,' replied Jeremiah, 'but there are a couple of things that I wanted to check with you. When we spoke before you said that you knew her, but you were clearly surprised that you were her only beneficiary. When she called to make the will I didn't see her; one of my junior colleagues spoke to her initially. It was only when you were mentioned as a beneficiary that it was brought to my attention; so after it had been drawn up, I saw her when she called to sign it. So how did you know her?'

'Jeremiah, you put me in a very difficult position. I don't want to answer that question. The time will come when I can and will answer it, but there is a reason why not at present. As far as the will is concerned, I was surprised to be named as a beneficiary because I thought someone else would be. I can't say who.'

'John, you are being very mysterious. I am your solicitor, I'm like a priest. I will keep your secrets.'

'You won't have to Jeremiah, because I am not going to tell them to you.'

'Well, tell me this. When I spoke to Miss Treacy she said she had been working for many years in France as a translator. Is your secret anything to do with that?'

'Jeremiah, I have told you. I am not saying anything.'

'One mystery you can solve, though. When she came to see me she asked about you, where you lived and so on. Did she ever contact you? Oh, and one more thing. When she was with me I noticed that she was wearing a glove on her left hand. It was a warm day and she had on a summer dress, but she kept the glove on all the time. I didn't like to ask why, but I was fascinated.'

'Jeremiah, how many times do I have to say it? I am not telling you anything, except to say that she did not contact me following her visit to you. I saw a piece in the *Gazette* about her death; who put that in?'

'That was us. It was a mistake because as we already knew you it was unnecessary. One of the juniors put it in. Anyway, no harm done. Now, one of the reasons I wanted to see you was to discuss what you want to do with the flat and her assets.'

'Can you sell the flat, put all the money together and send me a cheque when it's all done? That would seem the best way.'

'I think we can deal with all that, John. Do you want a memento of her?'

For a few moments John cast his mind back.

'No, thanks, I have absolutely everything I need. Just do the business and let me know. I promise that when the time is right you will know everything.'

Jeremiah Lewis stood up and shook hands with John.

'Thanks, John. I shall be in touch, but it will be a while yet.'

'Thank you Jeremiah. And I will keep my promise.'

John Williams left the building in deep thought. It was true what he had said to his solicitor; he had everything that he wanted from Mary. But one thing was troubling him, why was he her heir?

Chapter Fourteen

Fiona Lock dialled Madeleine's number. She was anxious to know how she had settled in, and wanted an update on her enquiries into the accident.

'Madeleine Porter speaking.'

'It's me,' said Fiona. 'How are you getting on? Settled in yet? Found anything out?'

'One at a time,' replied Madeleine, 'I'm fine and have settled in. I went into the town yesterday to do some shopping and to check out the church. While I was there I met this fellow who does stewarding, Ian Clay his name was. Nice chap.'

'Short work!' laughed Fiona, 'You haven't been there a week and you've found yourself a bloke already.'

'No, no. He said he was interested in local history and I was telling him about the Haven Horror Road story, which he already knew, of course. But he did say he would help if I wanted a hand with my investigations. He's in the church choir, so I shall see him tomorrow. I did look up the story in the local rag. There wasn't much more than the estate agent chap had told us. Just that the man was a bus driver named Stan Proctor, and his wife Edna was not in the car when it went over the cliff. There was one interesting bit, though. It said the body had not been found, and then four weeks later there was another report that said that the body had still not been found. There was no information about the wife at all.'

'Maybe she cut the brakes and he plunged over the cliff as a result,' said Fiona.

'Don't be silly. I am sure the police would have found out if that were the case. No, it looks as if it was what your old employer would have called an Act of God. I am going to have a look at the electoral roll for that period, though. It will be interesting to see how long they had lived at The Haven, and how long Mrs Proctor carried on living there afterwards.'

'How does this help with the clock?' asked Fiona.

'I have no idea. Probably not at all. Now, tell me your news. How are you? and how is the baby?'

'We're both fine. I am going for another scan on Monday. Just to check all is well.'

'It wasn't like that in my day,' said Madeleine, 'It was only with Damien, my youngest, that I had a scan at all, and that was one right at the beginning of the pregnancy. How many weeks are you now?'

'Six to go. I am feeling huge. Tim says he likes me like this, but I am beginning to feel very large and uncomfortable.'

'Look after yourself, and make sure that brother of mine does his share.'

'He is wonderful,' said Fiona, 'I couldn't ask for a more attentive husband and father-to-be. Victoria and Grace are coming to see us next weekend. It will be lovely to see them again; I do miss them.'

'Give them my love, won't you? Take care; I'll update you as to progress. I shall check the electoral registers as I said, and then, assuming that Stan and Edna are the couple involved, I shall search for their marriage details, and any children. I have nothing to connect them to the cuckoo clock, but I feel there is something there, I just don't know what. I am also going to advertise in the parish magazine, offering my services as a family historian. I tried it in Emberton and nothing came of it, but I might be more successful here. Nothing to do with Stan and Edna, only to keep me busy.'

'Sounds as if you are going to be busy enough. I am curious about this couple. Why didn't the wife pester the police about her missing husband? Maybe she was quite happy he was missing,' wondered Fiona.

'Yes, indeed. Hope you get on OK on Monday. Give my love to Tim, bye.'

'Bye.'

Fiona put the phone down; a worried frown across her face. She knew what raking up the past could bring.

Madeleine was pleased to have spoken to Fiona and to have caught up with her news. She was anything but worried; she was keen to get going. She couldn't check the electoral register until Monday, but the Internet is open twenty four hours a day, she thought. She logged on to her favourite family history website and searched for a marriage between a Stan Proctor and a woman named Edna. There it was; Stanley Proctor marrying Edna Fox in the spring of 1952 in Seatown. She decided to send for the marriage certificate to find out the full details. The marriage certificate would tell her where the marriage had taken place, where the couple were living at the time, and also the names and occupations of their respective fathers. Madeleine knew from experience that there was no telling when such information might come in useful. She wondered if they had had any children, although nothing had been mentioned in the accident report in the paper about children being left behind. So she searched for any children with the surname Proctor born to a woman with the maiden name of Fox, and she was successful once again. In the spring of 1955 a Paul Proctor was born in Seatown. Madeleine sent for the birth certificate as well. It would seem that if this was Edna's child, she was expecting at the time of the incident. Poor woman, pregnant with her first baby, and to have that happen to her husband.

She was excited by these discoveries, but she still could not see any connection to the cuckoo clock, and that was her main focus. Perhaps the two certificates and the electoral register would help, but she was unable to see how. Patience was a virtue she did have, unlike her brother, who wanted everything yesterday.

Tim had come into the room as Fiona was finishing her chat with Madeleine, and he saw the worried frown.

'What's the matter?' he asked.

'Nothing really. Madeleine was telling me what she was going to do about finding out more about this business involving the chap from her house; remember, the estate agent told us that tale about an accident. But then she went on about searching for details of the couple, and also any children. It worried me knowing what can turn up with such investigations.'

Fiona sniffed back the tears.

'Come here,' Tim said, as he took her in his arms, 'I am here for you, and nothing horrible is going to happen. Madeleine is much too sensible for that.'

He kissed her and held her tight, which made her feel so much better.

'This baby is coming between us,' she laughed, as she broke the embrace and pulled away. 'I can't get near enough to you.'

'I was telling Madeleine about the girls coming. I hope you don't mind but I miss them both very much. She sent her love to you and to them.'

'Of course I don't mind,' said Tim, 'I am looking forward to it. Now come and sit down and stop fretting. I have cooked something very special for you.'

Chapter Fifteen

Sunday morning dawned bright and cool and as Madeleine drove towards Seatown she inevitably thought again of Stan and Edna. They were still on her mind as she parked the car and walked towards St Martin's Church, just off the town square. As she walked into the churchyard, past the notice board, she saw the old man with the trilby hat whom she had seen the other day. He was sitting in the same place, dressed in the same way, huddled under a raincoat. Again she noticed him take out the notebook from his pocket.

She walked up to the church door, and as she did so she remembered Paul; I wonder where he is now. How old would he be? She did a quick calculation and then realised she didn't need to calculate anything; he was the same age as her. She looked round the congregation as she walked in. How many fifty-seven year old men were there here? She told herself not to be silly, and she settled into one of the chairs towards the back of the church. Shame about the chairs, she thought, I've always preferred pews.

As the choir processed to the stalls she had difficulty recognising Ian in his dark blue cassock, but he spotted her, caught her eye and smiled. The service was good, the hymns bright and the sermon interesting and a little challenging. She decided she could fit in here very nicely. At the end of the service the choir processed back to the vestry, and Madeleine joined the rest of the congregation in one of the side aisles, waiting for tea and coffee to be served.   One or two people spoke to her, asking if she was on holiday or visiting, and Madeleine explained how she had come to live outside the town, but she decided not to say where she was living; she didn't want a long chat about the Haven Horror.

'Morning Madeleine, glad you could come,' a familiar voice said behind her, and she turned to see the friendly face of Ian Clay.

''Hello, Ian, I nearly didn't recognise you in your robe. I enjoyed the service, and the choir's singing.'

'Thank you, at least for the compliment about the choir.   Mind you, it's always good when a newcomer praises the service generally.   Have you got yourself a drink? What would you like, tea or coffee?'

'Coffee please.'

Ian nudged his way through the crowd around the drinks table, picked up two coffees and a couple of biscuits and worked his way back to Madeleine.

'Biscuits not very exciting, I'm afraid.'

'That's fine, thank you.'

Ian eased his way over to some unoccupied chairs.

'Now, tell me what you have discovered. I know you went to the library, but have you had any more thoughts about what you found?'

Madeleine sat down and looked at Ian. She had always been good at judging character, and as a vicar's wife she often had the job of assessing people; informally of course, but Richard had found it very helpful on occasions. She considered Ian and wondered whether it would be appropriate to suggest he came to The Haven for a cup of tea and a chat about her discoveries, especially those she had made since she had seen him in the car park. What would his wife think? Where was she anyway? Maybe she should ask them both, but would that sound too formal?

'I have found out something else which might be helpful. Would you like to pop round this afternoon and we can share some ideas. Perhaps your wife would like to come as well? Three heads are better than two.'

'Thanks Madeleine. That sounds a good idea. Sadly my wife died three years ago after a long illness. As I said the other day, I would be very happy to help you in your quest, but I don't want to inflict myself on you.'

'I am sorry to hear about your wife. But I would like you to come.'

'In which case I shall. What time? About three? I have a book about local history which I will bring; it might shed some light on the subject.'

'Very good. I will see you later. You can park in front of the house off the road. Pull in by the barn and drive round.'

Madeleine downed her coffee

'Must go,' she said, 'I've got visitors this afternoon.'

'Oh well, I'd better not come then,' replied Ian, disappointedly.

'If you don't, I won't have any visitors, will I?'

She chuckled and slung her bag on to her shoulder and said goodbye. She was anticipating an interesting afternoon. It would be good to get a different point of view.

Madeleine stood up as she heard a car pull up outside the front window of the house. Ian Clay got out and looked around at the view. He was not a very tall man and his wispy grey hair blew in the breeze. Madeleine was pleased to see that he was dressed casually, in jeans and a short-sleeved shirt; unlike his 'Sunday best' that he had worn that morning. He turned back towards the house as she opened the front door.

'What a wonderful view you have here,' he said as he walked up the garden path.

'Yes, it is, especially in weather like this,' replied Madeleine. 'Do come in.'

She ushered Ian into the living room, where she had put out the copies of the newspaper reports, along with her laptop for easy access.

'My, my, that's a very splendid clock,' he said, gazing up at the cuckoo clock over the mantelpiece.

'It's not mine, but there is something of a mystery surrounding it. I'll tell you about it when we've got settled.'

She turned to go through into the kitchen.

'I'll put the kettle on. Tea OK? Do you have milk and sugar?'

'Yes, thanks. Milk please, no sugar.'

As Madeleine busied herself with the tea Ian looked around the room. It had been, as he had heard, done up, and was very smart. He imagined that the rest of the house would be the same, and, being nosy, he wandered through into the kitchen.

'Anything I can help you with?' he said.

'No. That's fine. You sit down and I will bring it through.'

She put the cups and saucers on a tray, together with some better biscuits than those on offer in church in the morning, which she had picked up on her way home.

'I'm not used to being waited on,' said Ian.

Madeleine guessed that as his wife had been ill for a long time, Ian had done much of the work around the house.

'My wife had a riding accident shortly after we were married, and she was in a wheelchair from that time on. We managed very well for a long time, but then in the last few years, she was able to do less and less because of her condition. Fortunately I was able to take early retirement from PPS so I could look after her.'

His eyes misted over as he remembered his wife and Madeleine thought it best to try to change the subject. She brought the tray through, having poured the tea in the kitchen, and put it down on a small side table.

'Biscuit?'

Ian accepted gratefully.

'Thanks. It is very good of you to ask me to come today. I did mean it the other day when I said about helping you with your investigations, I am very interested. So tell me, what have you got?'

Madeleine took a sip of tea and then showed Ian the copy newspaper reports.

'You probably know this already, but I was interested to find out the names of the couple who were living here at the time; Stan and Edna Proctor. What I thought was particularly interesting was that Stan was not found, and Edna didn't seem to care. Why not? On both counts.'

'As far as Stan is concerned,' replied Ian, 'I suppose it is possible that the body was washed out to sea and never found. If not, that means that he survived the fall. But if he survived then why didn't he go back home, or at least contact his wife to say he was OK? Otherwise, if he survived and was hurt, why didn't he go to hospital to be checked out? Presumably the police would have checked hospitals?'

'I don't think that he can have been washed out to sea. The sea usually washes bodies back up onto the shore, sooner or later, doesn't it? If he had gone to hospital, then the police would have traced him. In that case Stan Proctor is alive and well somewhere,' suggested Madeleine.

'Hold on,' said Ian, 'it was nearly sixty years ago. If he had survived, he'd be dead by now, wouldn't he?'

'Yes, I suppose so. What about Edna? If my husband had driven off in a storm, and I had been told that his car had been washed over the cliff and his body not found, I would have been badgering the police every day to find out what had happened. As she doesn't seem to have done that maybe we can assume that Edna was quite happy that Stan did not return. Now why would that be?'

'Sixty years on, it's difficult to know. What else have you found anyway? I got the impression you had more to tell me.'

'Before we get on to that, had you seen both the newspaper reports, the one four weeks later saying that no body had been found?'

'I hadn't seen the newspaper, but the local history book I told you about covers all of it pretty comprehensively. Why?'

'It struck me as being a bit like the dog that didn't bark in the night in the Sherlock Holmes story. You know, where Holmes says that the absence of the dog barking was very significant. Well, why did the newspaper report the absence of a body four weeks later? Clearly because they expected that a body would have been found by that time. It doesn't say so, but the inference is surely that something unexpected has happened to Stan Proctor. Also it says that Edna Proctor offered no comment. Isn't that odd?'

'Yes. It is. By the way, bearing in mind that Stan Proctor might still be alive, so might Edna.'

'So she might, and that brings me on to the other bits of information I have for you,' said Madeleine.

'For a number of years now I have being tracing my own family history, and sometimes other people's as well. In fact I am going to put an advert in the parish magazine offering my services, just to keep me out of mischief. Well, once I had found out from the newspaper the names of the couple, I checked on one of the family history websites I use to see if I could find details of their marriage.'

'I didn't know you could do that, isn't that information confidential?' queried Ian

'No, it's a matter of public record. Once you have identified the marriage on the indexes provided by the General Register Office, you can quote the reference number and buy a copy of the certificate for just under a tenner. So I looked for a marriage between a Stan Proctor and a woman named Edna, in or around Seatown. And I found one, Stanley Proctor marrying Edna Fox, in the second quarter of 1952. I think they are our couple, so I have ordered a copy of their marriage certificate, which will tell us exactly when and where they married, their ages, what their occupations were, and their fathers' names and occupations. Then I wondered if they had had any children, so I searched for the birth of someone called Proctor, born to a woman whose maiden name was Fox, and there he was; Paul, born in the spring of 1955.'

'Sorry, when did you say? Spring 1955? That means that...'

'Yes, she was pregnant at the time Stan disappeared. That wasn't in the papers.'

Madeleine paused and took another sip of tea. It was cold.

'All this excitement and I've let my tea go cold,' she said, 'what about yours?'

'Same,' said Ian, as he took a mouthful.

'I'll go and pour some more. I shall leave you to ponder.'

Madeleine went back into the kitchen with the cups. Meanwhile Ian sat thinking. There is more to this than first meets the eye. If Stan is still alive, and Edna, what about Paul? Surely that is even more likely. He would only be in his late fifties. Madeleine returned with the tea.

'I expect you have been thinking the same as me. Where is Paul, and does he know the answer? Anyway I have ordered Paul's birth certificate as well. They should both come later this week, I shall let you know.'

Madeleine felt very relaxed with Ian, and enjoyed sitting quietly drinking their second cup of tea, before it went cold as well.

'Thank you, Madeleine. Any more of those biscuits? They were delicious.'

Madeleine laughed; she liked this, a man who was comfortable enough with her to ask for more.

'I am sure I can find you some,' she said, walking out into the kitchen.

She returned with another plateful. Ian picked one up.

'Now what about this clock? You were going to tell me about it.'

'Yes, it's a very odd story. When I came down house-hunting the estate agents reluctantly gave me this house to look at. I am only renting it at present, and it appeared the owner was very particular who he was prepared to rent it out to. Eventually I met him here at the house, and when I walked into this room I commented favourably on the clock, as you did. Immediately he said I could have the house. He went on to tell me that the clock was his most treasured possession, and effectively he had bought this house and furnished it solely to accommodate the clock. It seems a strange thing to do.'

'Who is the owner, if you don't mind me asking?'

'A chap named John Williams. Local businessman, as far as I could gather.'

'Yes, he is. I know John Williams. He is the owner, and was the Chief Executive, of PPS where I used to work. He lives out at Steeple Morton, in a delightful thatched cottage. Very nice.'

'How long ago was that? That you were there?' asked Madeleine.

'Janice died three years ago, and I retired on a small pension a couple of years before that, so it must be five years. He had already stepped down as Chief Executive by then, but I was with the company for over twenty years, so I got to know him quite well. He was very hands-on where work was concerned. A lovely man, though. I always had the feeling that there was some sadness in his life, but no one knew anything of course.'

'Was he married?'

'Yes, not for very long though. He married his PA, Carole (with an e!), but she died about three years later; breast cancer so people said, but I don't know for sure.'

'That must be the sadness you mentioned then.'

'No,' replied Ian, 'I don't think so, I don't know why, but I feel there was more to it than that. But how does that have anything to do with this clock? Why is it his most treasured possession? What would make you value something beyond its price?'

'Something sentimental? A piece of jewellery or a book that reminds you of someone special. Baby clothes when your babies are grown-up,' suggested Madeleine.

'John Williams is a very successful businessman. His company is very well-respected and profitable. He has a beautiful house and I would guess a posh car. But he values a clock. Is it an antique?'

'I don't know much about antiques,' said Madeleine, 'I always imagine things on the *Antiques Roadshow* are more valuable than their experts say. I think if it were valuable he would have it at home; there is something extra about it that we don't know.'

'We need to find out then,' teased Ian, as the cuckoo appeared and gave the time as five o'clock.

'I'd better be going, it's been a very interesting afternoon, you certainly have work to do. Shall I leave my book here? You can let me have it back another time. I hope there will be another time.'

'There certainly will be,' said Madeleine, 'I will let you know when these certificates arrive, and I shall give more thought to John Williams and the clock. I'm so glad you could come.'

'Thank you again. Have you got my number? Let me jot it down for you.'

He scribbled his address and phone number on a pad by the phone.

'Thanks Ian, bye.'

She watched him as he drove away from the house and round the barn. I wonder what else he knows about John Williams, she thought; if he worked there for that long he must know more. Maybe he didn't realise what he knew.

Chapter Sixteen

The few days following Madeleine's afternoon with Ian flew by. She was busy getting herself settled in the house, and also exploring the surrounding area. She walked along the cliffs in the sunshine, and peered down from the edge on to the rocks below. She noticed the different rock formations and shapes, and tried to picture Stan and his car tumbling over the side. How frightening that would be, she thought. It was a still day with only small waves beating against the rocks, but it was a steady beat, and the rocks showed the effects of it in their odd shapes. She saw that there were small areas of rock which were horizontal and she tried to imagine a car falling and landing on such a piece. That would be very lucky and very unlikely, she thought, but there must be some way for Stan to have survived the fall. There was no way she could clamber down to the rocks and look upwards, which would have helped her to get a different perspective on the problem.

When she had moved to Seatown from Emberton she had not expected to be drawn into such a puzzle. She imagined pleasant walks along the cliffs, relaxing shopping in the town and time to please herself. She had submitted her advert for the family history research that she had mentioned to Ian, and she was told that would be delivered around the town next week. She had, fortunately, just caught the deadline. But before that she needed to sort out this conundrum of the Proctors and the puzzle of the clock. She still felt that there was a connection between the two.

She wondered how long the clock had been in the house. Who were the previous owners? Maybe she should find out and ask them. The estate agents had said it had been a holiday let before John Williams had bought it. Perhaps they were local and she could ask them. She decided to speak to Clive Redding at Tomkins and Snell.

With these thoughts racing through her mind she had not realised it had started to rain. She took out her cagoule and put it on, struggling to get it over her head. The wind suddenly got up and as she turned for home the cliffs and the rocks below looked much less inviting. Keeping a safe distance from the edge she hurried back, and was pleased to get to the safety of her own home as the rain got harder. She took off the wet cagoule and hung it over the shower tray to dry off and put the kettle on for a hot drink.

She sat down to think: Clive Redding. That's what she was going to do; phone him. She checked the number and rang.

'Good afternoon, Tomkins and Snell, how can I help you?'

She recognised Samantha's voice.

'Hello Samantha, it's Madeleine Porter here. Is Mr Redding free?'

'Yes, he is. I'll call him for you.'

She called across to Clive who picked up the phone.

'Hello Mrs Porter, Clive Redding here. What can I do for you?'

'Just a bit of information about the house. I think you said that the house had been a holiday let for many years. I know it's a bit of a cheek, but I was wondering if you could tell me who the owners were. There's something I wanted to ask them, and I don't want to trouble Mr Williams with it.'

'I am sure you will understand that I cannot disclose that sort of information,' said Clive, 'but what I can tell you is that the owners of The Haven before Mr Williams were a couple who live in Jersey, and have lived there for many, many years. I believe they inherited it from either his or her father. I never met them, and I used to deal with them by letter or on the phone. You will appreciate that I can't give you their names and address.'

'I understand. I was hoping to discover whether the cuckoo clock in the living room was here in their day or not. It was only nosiness really.'

'I can tell you that,' replied Clive, and Madeleine was suddenly hopeful. What was he going to tell her?

'When the house was put up for sale Mr Williams bought it immediately, without seeing it. I then met him at the property when he had completed his improvements and redecorations. The clock was not there then. I remember because he said he was going to bring a cuckoo clock when he saw potential tenants, and I thought it very unusual, to say the least.'

Madeleine was encouraged. This was the first bit of information about the clock she had heard from someone other than John Williams. She decided to press a little more.

'So he owned the clock before he owned the house? He told me it belonged here. That's funny isn't it?'

Clive was not to be pushed.

'I'm sorry, Mrs Porter, but I can't say any more. I have probably said too much already. Please don't mention what I have said to Mr Williams.'

'No, of course I won't.'

Madeleine sensed that Clive knew a lot more than he was telling. Maybe she would try another day. She put down the handset and sat back in the armchair. Why did he own the clock before the house if it belonged there? One to ask Ian, she thought.

The following morning the post brought the two certificates that Madeleine had ordered at the weekend. She slit open the envelopes, intrigued what she was going to discover. She looked at the marriage certificate first; it was quite straightforward. The marriage of Stanley William Proctor, age 32, bachelor, bus driver, of 39, Lime Street, Seatown, to Edna Fox, age 19, spinster, shop assistant, of 2 Rathbone Street, Seatown, at St Martin's Church, Seatown on 31 May 1952; fathers' names David Proctor, labourer , and William Fox, deceased. That all seemed perfectly above board. What about Paul Proctor's birth? She looked at the certificate. Again it was very ordinary; birth of Paul Proctor on 2 April 1955 at The Haven, Seatown. Mother's name Edna Proctor formerly Fox, father's name Stanley Proctor, bus driver, deceased.

Maybe not so ordinary after all, thought Madeleine. Edna had registered the birth and described Stanley as being dead. Did she know this or was it guesswork? Or perhaps, she wondered, it was wishful thinking.

Working on the basis that Edna had said Stan was dead, Madeleine went back to her computer to find the death record; and then she could order the certificate and find out the full details. She searched for anyone called Proctor dying between 1952 and 2006, the most recent date available online, thinking she might find Edna as well. She was surprised when she found neither Stan nor Edna, but she was more surprised when she found the death of Paul Proctor, age 0, in the fourth quarter of 1955 in Seatown.

Madeleine was quite shocked at her discovery of the death of Paul. She knew that infant mortality in the Victorian era was high, but, as we all do, she imagined that it was a thing of the past, even in the 1950s. Once again she ordered the certificate to see the circumstances surrounding little Paul's death. The cause of death would be interesting, as would the address at which he died, and who registered the death. All these factors would help Madeleine to build up a picture of life at The Haven during Edna's time there. She rang Ian and told him about the certificates she had already received, and they agreed to meet up when the latest one arrived.

While she was waiting, over the next few days, her thoughts went back to Emberton and Fiona and Tim. Fiona's time was drawing near and she, Madeleine, was getting very excited. She could imagine what Tim would be like, the same as he had been since that day that Fiona said to him 'I'm pregnant'. Walking on air. She considered ringing her friend and telling her of the latest developments, but thought that maybe she had enough on her mind without family history mysteries.

The familiar white envelope appeared on the mat a few mornings later. She opened it eagerly. The death certificate of Paul Proctor made very sad reading; he died aged five months, on 20 October 1955, the cause of death was poliomyelitis. Edna had registered the death, which had occurred at the District General Hospital, which had since closed, on the outskirts of Seatown. Madeleine remembered polio being mentioned as a feared disease, although she was too young to have known this for herself. She wondered when the polio vaccine had become available as she had a feeling it was round about the same time. Upon investigation she discovered that it was first announced in 1955. Little Paul was therefore especially unlucky, as his death occurred shortly before the mass immunisation project had started which virtually eradicated the disease.

Madeleine sat down and considered what she had discovered. Stan and Edna Proctor had been married in 1952 and moved to the cliff-side cottage known as The Haven. In August 1954, Stan had disappeared after an incident in which his car was pushed over a cliff. Edna was expecting a baby at the time of Stan's disappearance, and had her baby in April 1955. He died five months later, of polio. Did Edna stay at The Haven? If not where did she go, and why? And how is the cuckoo clock related to all these events, if at all? Madeleine was certain that it was related, but she needed to find out more about Stan and Edna to unlock that mystery. She rang Ian. It was time for them to consider what to do next.

'Electoral registers.'

It was Sunday afternoon and Ian and Madeleine had got together for another of their consultations.

'Sorry? What did you say?' asked Madeleine.

'Electoral registers,' repeated Ian. 'When we spoke on the phone and you gave me a very succinct summary of your findings, you said you wanted to find out what happened to Edna and how long she stayed at The Haven. The electoral registers, old ones of which are held at the county record office, list the voters in all the houses in any particular year. If you look up The Haven, you will see which voters were living here. The registers are compiled in the October of the previous year, so they are not absolutely accurate, but it might help.'

'So what you are saying is that if we look up The Haven for 1954 we should find Stan and Edna Proctor listed as voters at this address. Then we check for 1955 and so on, until the names of the occupants change.'

'Yes, that's right. But don't forget that the voting age in 1954 was twenty one. How old was Edna?'

'On the marriage certificate it said she was nineteen; that was in 1952, so twenty one in 1954. That would be the first year in she would have been eligible to vote,' said Madeleine.

'That reminds me,' said Ian. 'If Edna was nineteen when she got married, she would have needed parental consent. Age of majority, for getting married as well as with voting, was twenty one. Does that mean that her parents should have witnessed the marriage certificate, because they didn't?'

'According to the certificate her father was dead. Mother would have had to give consent. I know when Richard was faced with this, and in recent years it was much rarer, he would visit the parents to make sure they were aware of what their son or daughter was doing. Sometimes he would get them to sign a form so that he had consent in writing, but I don't think that was a legal necessity. In any event it would not be necessary for them to be witnesses on the certificate. Anyway, what you are saying is that we should go to the record office and look at the register for 1954 and onwards. That will give us a clearer picture of life at The Haven. But if she leaves there is no way of knowing where she went, is there?'

'No, because it is done by addresses. Shall we go together? Have a day trip to Dorchester?'

'Sounds good, how about tomorrow? Now, would you like another cup of tea and a quality biscuit?'

'You have found my weakness. Thank you.'

Ian took the plate with the biscuits and sat in silence while Madeleine went to pour some more tea. He was enjoying this new friendship; the tea, the biscuits, the chat and the mysteries. He looked again at the cuckoo clock, begging it silently to reveal its secrets. As Madeleine came back with the tea, he wondered if they had been wrong and there were none. Tomorrow's trip might prove critical.

Chapter Seventeen

It had been three weeks since Eric Smith had died, and Tina Jenkins and her partner Kevin had completed all the necessary arrangements, including a small service at the local crematorium. Unfortunately the funeral had to be delayed because Kevin was away on a youth leaders' course which he couldn't get out of. Tina had said that she thought her father would have liked a Christian funeral, so the duty minister, who that day was the vicar of St Martin's Church in Seatown, had conducted a service for them. The flowers were minimal, just a small posy from Tina and Kevin, 'for Dad'.

On their way home Tina said how disappointed she was that no one else had come.

'Who else is there who could have come?' Kevin asked her, 'I don't know much about your family, but I had always understood that he was an only child, and you were his only child.'

'Yes, that's right. I suppose I had wondered whether Mum might have come. I know they were divorced years ago, but she might have thought she should come.'

'Did you tell her that your Dad had died?'

'Yes, well, I sent a letter to the last address I had of hers. Mind you we haven't had a Christmas card for about three years. Maybe the ones I have been sending to the

Dorchester address haven't been finding her. It's a shame about Jimmy. He would have come if he had been at home. I don't think there is anyone else.'

'No friends?'

'No. Of course at his age most of his contemporaries will have died anyway. There was no one at the home he made friends with. Brenda didn't come; I thought she might have come too. But that's all.'

When they arrived back home there was a magazine on the doormat.

'*St Martin's Mission Magazine*,' she said contemptuously. 'Why do they send this to us?'

'I usually scan through it then put it in the recycling. It goes to every house in the parish,' said Kevin, trying to calm her down. 'Sometimes it has useful adverts in it, if nothing else. You know, local tradesmen, plumbers, odd-job men, that type of thing.'

Tina picked it up and glanced through the pages, full of church activities and information; none of it of any interest to Tina. She skimmed through the adverts that Kevin had mentioned and noticed one, which she read out to him;

'What about this then, Kevin. "How well do you know your family? Would you like a hand in tracing your family tree? Friendly advice is available from Madeleine Porter. First hour free, then £15 per hour. Telephone

Seatown 653927''. We could look up Dad. I've always been puzzled about his earlier life. What do you think?'

'I think £15 per hour is more than we can afford. Can we have the free hour without committing to the rest, do you think?'

'Might be able to. But do you think it is a good idea?'

'Before we do that,' said Kevin, 'just remember, you might not like what you find. I met someone through work who said his father had gone in for this, and wished he hadn't. He discovered one of his grandfathers had hanged himself. Quite shocked him.'

'I don't think that Dad has anything like that in his background.'

'Neither did Les, this bloke from work's dad. That's the problem, you never know.'

Tina thought about the receipt from the shop, and the envelope which they had found in the old box that Brenda had given her to bring home from The Laurels.

'This Madeleine Porter might be able to help with that shop receipt and the number in the envelope. Also when I registered the death they asked me when he was born, so I told them, but I have never seen a copy of his birth certificate. Funny that, you'd have thought it would be with the other papers from the home.'

'Why don't I give her a ring and find out exactly what she is offering. If possible we'll go for the free hour and take it from there. We can ask her about the other things at the same time.'

Kevin punched in the numbers.

'Hello, Madeleine Porter speaking.'

'Hello Mrs Porter, I'm Kevin Jenkins. My partner and I have seen your advert in the *Mission Magazine* about family history.'

'Yes,' replied Madeleine, keenly, 'how can I help?'

'I see that you say that you do an hour free and then charge £15 per hour. It's a bit pricy for us. Can we just have the free hour?'

'Yes, of course. What I usually do is to have a chat first to find out what you know already, and what you want to find out. Then I can make an estimate of how long it is likely to take, and then you can decide what you want to do.'

'So, as well as tracing the family tree do you do other enquiries? My partner's father has died very recently, and there were one or two oddments left behind which we don't understand. I thought perhaps you might be able to help.'

'I will certainly try, Kevin. Can I call you Kevin? Thanks. Now what is your partner's name? Tina. And she is Jenkins as well? Right. Why don't we make an appointment for you and Tina to come and see me at home, and we will have a look at what there is to do? If I can take your address and phone number; thanks. Now when would suit you best?'

'How about tomorrow evening?' suggested Kevin,' seven o'clock be OK?'

Madeleine agreed. She was very excited that the advert had brought such a quick response. She wondered what she might uncover about Tina's dad. Probably nothing, but there was always hope.

She had given Kevin explicit directions where to find her and where to park, but as a local man he was well aware of the location of The Haven. That story of Stan certainly hung around the house, but as had been said, it was probably the most exciting thing ever to happen in Seatown.

She welcomed them in and sat them down in the living room. Tina was looking anxious, and had taken her shoes off, apologetically, at the front door. Kevin was a more confident young man, and when he said that he was a youth work leader, she understood why. Bringing through a tray with tea and biscuits she tried to make them feel comfortable, but it was hard-going with Tina, who was clearly intimidated by the house and its furnishings.

'Let me explain,' said Madeleine, and she told them about her background and how she had become interested in family research. She told them that there was no obligation after their free hour, and that anything she discovered would be confidential, unless, of course, it was criminal.

'Oh, I don't think that Dad did anything like that!' exclaimed Tina.

'No, no,' pacified Madeleine, 'I wasn't suggesting that he had, but I have to tell   everybody that. Anyway you say that he died recently. Shall we start there?'

Tina began, hesitantly;

'My dad's name was Eric Smith and he was born on twenty third of November in 1919. He married my Mum, Sylvia Harris she was, in 1965 and I was born in 1967. I am an only child and Mum and Dad divorced in 1993. I don't know whether Mum remarried or not and we have now lost touch. So you see he was quite old when he married Mum, whether he had ever been married before I don't know. He never spoke of anyone else, but then he wasn't much of a one for talking at all. He died at The Laurels nursing home on eighth of May, three weeks ago. He had a stroke three years ago so it was very difficult talking to him. Very often I wonder whether he even knew I was there, and then occasionally he would burst out with something that made no sense at all.'

'So what would you like me to find out for you? Grandparents, or do you know those?'

'No, I don't. I suppose because Dad was old it didn't sort of crop up. It would be interesting to know, whether they were local, that sort of thing.'

'When I spoke to Kevin on the phone yesterday he said that you had some things of your Dad's you didn't understand. What were they?'

Madeleine was convinced that neither Tina nor Kevin was too bothered about building their family tree. Their interest, she thought, was more particular.

Tina opened the small bag she had brought with her;

'It was these,' she said, handing them to Madeleine. 'When we went to the nursing home after Dad died, they gave us a box of his belongings, not very much for a whole life, but... '

Tina started to cry as she recalled that visit. Madeleine poured her some more tea and Kevin put a consoling arm around her.

'It's OK, there's no rush,' said Madeleine. 'Take your time.'

Tina dried her eyes and started again;

'In the box were lots of bits and pieces of paper, bills, that sort of thing. Nothing of any value or interest. But then we found this.'

She handed the torn receipt to Madeleine.

'It's very old as you can see. The price for whatever it was for is in old money and I don't know how much that is.'

'19/11d,' said Madeleine, 'in old money there were twenty shillings in a pound, and twelve pence in a shilling. So whatever this was for cost just under a pound. In the same way that you would see today something priced at 99p. But don't forget that in, when was it, 1952, a pound was worth much more than it is today.'

'Have you heard of this shop, Lawrence and James?'

'No, but then I only moved here a month ago. If you want to leave it with me I will make some enquiries. There will be some people around who know what type of shop it was.'

'The other thing which we found was this old envelope. We very nearly threw it away. Inside the envelope was this piece of paper.'

She handed it over to Madeleine who looked at an old piece of what looked like writing pad paper with a number on it. 1510.

'Does this mean anything to you at all?' she asked.

Kevin interrupted. 'We have absolutely no idea whatsoever. Is it a code for something, a combination lock number? We have puzzled over it ever since we found it, and keep coming up with more and more outrageous answers.'

''Tell me some,' said Madeleine.

'As I said, a code, a combination lock, a date. If you hold it up to the mirror it looks like 2021, that could be something. How about a Swiss bank account number?'

'Now that is wishful thinking,' laughed Tina.

Madeleine suggested that they leave the receipt and the paper with the number with her. She would trace the shop, she didn't think that would be very difficult, and ponder the number. She wondered if Ian might have some ideas. She said she would also trace Eric's parents.

Kevin and Tina thanked Madeleine as they left, comforted by Madeleine's obvious interest in their problems. Madeleine turned back to look at the paper again; and one or two ideas came to mind.

Chapter Eighteen

Madeleine's trip with Ian to the record office in Dorchester had to be postponed when they realised that it was closed on Mondays. Ian was on stewarding duty on the Tuesday so they rearranged their day out for Wednesday. As far as Madeleine was concerned this had been very convenient because in the meantime she had spoken to Tina and Kevin, and she could ask Ian what he thought about the receipt; indeed he may even know the answer.

She made an early start because of the parking and traffic, stopping off in Seatown to pick up Ian. The record office closed at lunchtimes and they had planned to explore the records first, and then have some lunch and a wander around the town. Fortunately they were able to find a space at the very small car park at the record office. Madeleine was enjoying having some company in her explorations; just having someone to share her thoughts with was very helpful.

She completed the registration form which gave them access to the records and asked for the electoral registers for 1952 through to 1956 for The Haven. The assistant explained that it would be in one of the Seatown registers and they would have to browse through them to find the address. She handed Madeleine six fat volumes, much thumbed, and to Madeleine's untrained eye, in no particular order. Starting with the 1952 volume she flicked through the pages, and eventually found what she was looking for:

The Haven – George and Maureen Stapleton.

'Who are they?' she asked Ian. 'Where are Stan and Edna?'

'Don't forget that the registers are compiled in the October of the previous year. So in October 1951 George and Maureen Stapleton must have been living there and would have completed the forms.'

'Stan and Edna married in May 1952, didn't they? So presumably the Stapletons left or died, leaving it available for the Proctors.'

'Let's have a look at 1953, then. Stan should have filled in the forms in October 1952, so are they there?' said Ian.

'I notice you said Stan would have filled in the form; still I suppose in those days it would have been the job of the man of the house to do such things,' replied Madeleine.

Madeleine picked up the volume marked 1953 and searched again.

'Here we are,' she said triumphantly, 'Stanley William Proctor, living at The Haven.'

'That's odd. Where's Edna? Maybe Stan didn't think she was up to voting.'

'Ian, what a dreadful thing to say. You don't know anything about the man. Anyway how old was Edna? I don't think she was old enough to vote. On her marriage certificate it said she was nineteen. That was in May 1952. In that case she wouldn't be twenty one, which was the voting age in those days, until 1954. That's why she's not there.'

'Sorry, Madeleine. Yes, you're right,' conceded Ian.

'So the 1954 volume should show them both,' said Madeleine, 'let's check.'

She opened it and turned the pages and found the entry.

'There you are, Stanley and Edna Proctor. Just as they should be.'

Madeleine took out a notebook she had brought with her and a pencil. She jotted down the details of the Stapletons and Proctors. She was thinking about the clock, because that is what this was all about.

'The next volume should be interesting,' said Ian. 'If Stan did disappear in August 1954 has Edna filled in a form in October for the following year?'

The answer was yes, and in the register for 1955 only Edna was shown living at The Haven. Madeleine had told Ian about the birth and death of little Paul, and bearing in mind that the death occurred in late October, they surmised that Edna would have filled the forms in that year.

So when they opened the 1956 edition they were very surprised to find that the property was not listed at all.

'Does that mean that she just hadn't filled in the form, or that it was actually empty?' asked Madeleine.

'I don't know, but it does make you wonder. If she filled in the form the year before, why not again? If she didn't fill in the form, would she be retained on the voting list anyway? It would seem not, but maybe she told the council she was leaving and so they delisted the property because no one else had registered as living there.'

'Her little baby had died that same month; perhaps she was too distressed to bother with forms,' said Madeleine.

'It is not helping us though, is it? If Edna was still living at The Haven after Paul died she might have registered the following year. We need to look at 1957. I'll ask to have a look at that one. If she is not there I think we can assume she has left. I suppose it is possible she remarried and is living elsewhere.'

'Hang on, Ian. We have not found Stan dying yet. One step at a time.'

Ian collected the books together and returned them to the assistant at the desk.

'Can I see the register for 1957, please?'

'Yes, thanks for returning these, I'll go and get 1957 for you. Were you successful in what you were looking for?'

'Only partly,' replied Ian, 'the woman seems to disappear in 1956 and the property is not listed. Does that mean she didn't fill in a form? Or would she be retained even without a form?'

'The absence of the address from the electoral register means no more or less than that no one has completed the form saying that they are living there. They may still live there and not be eligible to vote, or may have just forgotten.'

'I will check 1957 anyway, if I may?'

The clerk went away and got the book for Ian to look at. He took it back to the table and he and Madeleine saw that in 1957 there was a Frederick Cummings listed.

'Well, that's that,' said Madeleine, 'Edna has gone. Next question, where to? And is any of this relevant to the clock mystery which is what I am meant to be solving?'

'We need to think further on that, over lunch I would suggest. Our work here is done for the time being.'

Ian returned the book and they signed out. A pleasant, warm breeze greeted them as they emerged from the stuffy offices. Turning a corner they spotted an attractive cafe serving interesting lunches, with pavement chairs and tables. They sat down and perused the menu, from which Ian chose the chicken and apricot sandwiches and Madeleine, the brie and mushroom tart. A young waitress, whom Madeleine thought looked no more than twelve, came to take their order, which Ian placed, asking for coffee for Madeleine and tea for himself.

While they were waiting for the food to be served they contemplated their discoveries of the morning.

'Stan and Edna were there after they married and all seemed fine,' said Madeleine, 'then what happened next? Stan disappears, and I have looked to see if I can find the death, without success. So he is a mystery, and then Edna vanishes as well.'

'Have you checked to see if Edna marries again?' asked Ian. 'That would account for her not being there.'

'Yes, it would, but if Stan is not dead she can't marry again.'

'She can,' countered Ian, 'but she shouldn't.'

'But you imagine, if Edna got married again, so soon after Stan's disappearance, with no absolute certainty of his death, wouldn't someone raise an objection at that bit in the marriage service? It would be too risky, although I suppose she could have gone somewhere totally different where no one knew her.'

'We know she is still in Seatown in October 1955 because that's when Paul dies. After that it's anyone's guess. She may have wanted to get away because the house and the area held too many bad memories for her.

By the way, do you think that Stan even knew she was pregnant?'

'Count the months,' said Madeleine, 'it's very close. Women tended to leave it much longer sixty years ago before confirming pregnancy. These days it can be within a few days, but I know my Mum told me she was three months with me before she was sure. No DIY pregnancy tests at Boots in those days.'

'No, that's true. I was thinking that if Stan knew, and he survived the fall, wouldn't he have come back to see Edna and his baby?'

The sandwiches and tart arrived and they looked delicious. On tasting them, both Madeleine and Ian said the food was as good as it looked.

'You would certainly think so,' said Madeleine, in between mouthfuls. 'But wouldn't you also think that even when she was pregnant, never mind when the baby was born, Edna would have wanted to let him know?'

'Well, know or not, it seems clear that Stan never returned.'

'Would you like another coffee, Madeleine?' asked Ian.

'Yes, thanks, it was lovely; food and drink.'

Ian called the waitress over and ordered a coffee for Madeleine, and poured himself another cup of tea.

'What were the other things?' he asked. 'You said that Tina and Kevin had other questions they wanted you to investigate.'

'The receipt and the envelope,' replied Madeleine. 'When Tina's father died recently the nursing home gave her a box of personal possessions; nothing very much, but there were two items which Tina could not understand. One was a receipt from a shop in Seatown, Lawrence and James, dated twenty third of May 1952 for something costing 19/11d. The details of the purchase had been torn away. Tina didn't know what it was for or why her dad had kept it. She wanted to know if I could find out what sort of shop it was. I said that as I was new I had no idea, but that I would find out. Have you ever heard of them?'

'No, I've lived and worked in the town since the early eighties, and I don't remember any shop of that name. I can think of some people at church who would know. I will ask around.'

'Thanks, I am sure they would welcome that. What do Lawrence and James sound like to you?'

'I don't know, tailors maybe, or furniture shop? Difficult to guess. What would have cost 19/11d in 1952? Leave it with me; I shall ask one or two old ladies I know. Now what was the other? What envelope?'

'Inside the box they gave to her was an envelope, and inside the envelope was this piece of paper.'

She handed the paper with the number 1510 written on it, to Ian.

'What do you make of that?'

Ian peered closely at the paper.

'It's lined, very faint, like that old-fashioned writing paper. Written in pen, not ball point. There's also a watermark.'

He held the paper up to the light.

'No. It's not a watermark, but a stain where the paper has got wet. Have you got the envelope?'

'Yes, here you are.'

Madeleine handed it over to him and he gazed intently at it. Holding the paper and the envelope together he again held them up to the light.

'I don't think they match,' he said, 'I think the envelope is not the same style as the paper. There is also a slight colour difference. The paper is tinged with blue, but the envelope is quite white. I would suggest that the paper was written on at one time and then put into the envelope on another occasion. The fact that the paper is lined, and that the number is written in ink not biro, suggests that it is quite old. Not many people these days use fountain pens, particularly for casual scribbling like this number.'

'What wonderful deduction,' Madeleine said admiringly, 'I'm so glad I brought you along.'

She laughed and put her hand on his arm.

'Next question is, what does it mean?' she said.

'That is much more difficult. A random number written on a piece of paper could be anything. Do you know, or rather does Tina know, for certain, that her father wrote the number? Is it his handwriting?'

'I don't know, and Tina didn't say.'

Then Madeleine caught the eye of the waitress who was watching them and hoping to be able to clear the table.

'Sorry,' she said to her, 'come on Ian, I think we need to go.'

Ian looked up and realised what she was saying.

'I am so sorry,' he said to the waitress.

They paid the bill and left promptly.

Walking back to the car Ian continued to ponder the number. Without further information he did not think that he could offer any more suggestions. He thought it would have been written too long ago for it to be a PIN number, Tina's father was not the type to have a numbered Swiss bank account, or a safety deposit box at a bank. If it was a date then what was on the fifteenth of May, and which year anyway?

Madeleine dropped him back home and thanked him for an enjoyable day, and he agreed that he had enjoyed it as much as she had. He said he would continue to think about the number, and he would make enquiries about the shop receipt. Madeleine drove home more puzzled than ever.

The following day was one of Ian's stewarding days at the church. He usually arrived about half past nine, unlocked the doors, and set out the stands with the various information and sale items about the church. There was a small kitchen where he could make himself a hot drink, and during the day he would meet and greet visitors to the town who were interested in churches, either architecturally or spiritually, and sometimes both. He also met various members of the congregation who came in on different days to do their bit towards keeping the whole enterprise going. Sometimes it would be the flower ladies (and always ladies Ian had noticed), sometimes cleaners and occasionally one or both churchwardens in pursuit of their duties. The vicar would also pop in from time to time.

Today was a Thursday and that was brass cleaning day. Jean Sanders had cleaned the brass in St Martin's Church for as long as anyone could remember. She took delight in cleaning and polishing the brass candlesticks on the high altar, the eagle lectern and the smaller candlesticks on the side aisle altars. She also cleaned and polished the brass tops to the churchwardens' staves. Once done she would stand back and admire her handiwork, the brass gleaming in the sunlight, with not a fingerprint in sight. Then she would say;

'It's all for the Lord.'

She said nothing more and nothing less; it was the same every week. Ian was very tempted to join in, but thought it would be unkind. However this week he did want to speak to her before she left, and so after she had completed her ritual he called to her;

'Jean. Just before you go, I have a question for you.'

Jean bristled and was ready to defend herself.

'Nothing to do with church,' he said, 'I was talking to a friend yesterday, and she said that she thought at one time there was a shop in the town called Lawrence and James. I said I had never heard of them, but you have been here longer than me. Have you heard of them?'

Jean smiled a broad gap-toothed smile. She was a short woman in her mid to late seventies, carrying more weight than was probably good for her, and with iron-grey hair cut bluntly. Her clothes were ordinary, to be kind, and her shoes down-at heel. She had been a widow for many years, and no one ever mentioned Mr Sanders.

'Lawrence and James, well, well, well. It's a long time since I've heard them mentioned. When my sister and I were young we would stand and look in their window on our way home from school, choosing which rings our future husbands would buy for us. All too expensive though. They were jewellers. Next door to the baker's shop I think they were. Closed down years ago, though. I think the owner ran off with one of the assistants, terrible scandal at the time. When was that? Late sixties I should think.'

'How expensive was expensive?' said Ian, eager to find out as much as possible.

'You must remember inflation, young Ian. Most of it was over five pounds I recall. My sister and I would have been looking in the window late forties, so that was a lot of money then.'

'Nothing as cheap as 19/11d, then?'

'No, I don't think so. Can't really remember, might have been sometimes.'

Ian thanked her for her help and Jean went her way, inwardly smiling at the memory of her and Violet looking in that jeweller's window all those years ago. It had been such fun and so innocent.

Chapter Nineteen

Since Madeleine's move to Seatown her daily routine had changed significantly. When she was a 'working' vicar's wife, and then when she had moved in with Tim, she had been a light sleeper and an early riser. Whether it was being on her own in the house, or the sea air she didn't know, but she now found she needed a good eight hours sleep, and was rarely up and about before half past eight.

It was, therefore, with some surprise that she was woken at quarter past six in the morning the day after her trip to Dorchester with Ian. The phone ringing at that time of day rarely brought good news. She picked up the handset by the bed and said blearily;

'Hello.'

'Madeleine.'

It was Tim. She then guessed why the phone had rung so early.

'Tim, what is it? How's Fiona?'

She sat up in bed, now fully awake.

'She's fine, well, I think so. I'm at the hospital in Emberton. We went to bed early, then I brought her in last night about one o'clock. She woke up with terrible pains. She thought she was going into labour so I rushed her here.'

'And?' said Madeleine.

'She's two weeks early but the hospital seem to think that the little one is on the way.'

'How exciting. Have you been there all night?'

'Yes I have. I spoke to the midwife just before ringing you and she said she thought it would be another couple of hours at most. All is going well and Fiona is OK. I have sent a text to the girls so that they know what's going on. Madeleine, I am so thrilled, I can't tell you.'

'Calm down, Tim. I'll get up and dressed and come up if you would like me to. Would Fiona like me to, do you think?'

'I'm sure she would, but I will go and ask her.'

'Text me. I'll probably be in the shower.'

Madeleine put the phone down and got out of bed. She showered, dressed and sat down to some breakfast. She thought she would need some sustenance for what promised to be a very busy and exciting day. She had seen that Tim had sent her a text saying that Fiona would be delighted to see her, which pleased her. Since meeting Fiona she had felt a sisterly bond between them, although she was considerably older. She thought back to the births of her own babies, five of them. It was such a lovely time having them tiny and helpless, gazing up at you, with unconditional love. She and Richard had had five sons, so she was secretly hoping for a little girl, but she knew that

Fiona and Tim had requested not to be told the sex of the baby when they had had the scans.

It was grey and overcast as Madeleine set out for Emberton. By the time she had left it was the busiest time of the day, so the journey was slow. When she was about halfway there her phone beeped on the passenger seat. It was a message from Tim. She looked anxiously for a lay-by so she could stop and read the message. She saw the familiar blue sign indicating parking one mile ahead. She pulled in and stopped the car, picking up the phone with trembling hands. She read the message;

'Welcome to Joseph, seven pounds twelve ounces. Mother and baby doing well, not sure about Dad. See you soon take care. Love from all three of us.'

For a fleeting moment she felt a twinge of disappointment, another boy, but she was also delighted. She replied;

'Well done Mum, and Dad, and welcome Joseph. Love to all. See you soon.'

She wiped a tear away from the corner of her eye and turned the key in the ignition. She mustn't rush now, take it steady. The traffic eased and she made her way to the County Hospital on the outskirts of Emberton. Parking in one of the bays she thought how scandalous it was that relatives had to pay to visit ill loved ones. It had made her blood boil when these car parking charges had first been introduced, and it made her equally cross every time she came across them. But she could do nothing about them and she grudgingly took a ticket from the machine.

She walked into the main entrance of the hospital and scanned the notice board for directions to Maternity. Then she was enveloped by a huge hug from behind. Startled she tried to turn around.

'I've just come downstairs to see if you were here.'

Tim's voice reassured her.

'Come on, up here'

He took his sister's hand and raced her up three flights of stairs.

'Hold on, Tim,' said Madeleine, 'I'm too out of condition to run up stairs like this.'

'They're in here,' he said, not listening. He pulled her through the doors into a room with four beds, each screened from the other with curtains. Going to the first set of curtains he pulled them back and there was Fiona, sitting up, looking deliriously happy, with a tiny bundle in her arms, with dark brown hair sticking up like a Mohican.

'Joseph,' announced Tim, proudly, 'and Fiona, of course.'

Madeleine hugged Fiona and kissed her, and then kissed Joseph.

'Hello, Joseph, welcome to the family.'

Fiona was smiling and crying at the same time. She could not remember being so happy.

'Is everything OK?' asked Madeleine.

'Yes,' replied Fiona, 'it all went like clockwork. I came in at one o'clock; they checked me over, said that things were moving and left me to it. A couple of hours later they returned and then kept an eye on me. And this little chap was born at quarter past ten. You arrived in perfect time. Unlike when you were having yours, though, I don't think they keep you in, as long as everything has gone to plan. I will be out by teatime. All is ready at home so that isn't a problem.'

'I think you need to get some rest beforehand. I'll take Tim home and he can have a snooze and a bite to eat. You do the same if you can. Remember, today is the last day you can rest for the next twenty years at least,' advised Madeleine.

She kissed Fiona and Joseph again and pulled Tim up out of the bedside chair where he was gently dozing.

''Come on, Dad, time to go home and have a rest.'

Tim stood up, hugged and kissed his wife and son and walked down the corridor to the stairs, as if on air.

'We will be back later on this afternoon. I'll ring the ward to make sure you are OK to come home,' called Madeleine back to Fiona as they left.

Madeleine paid the car park ticket, and for once was not irritated by it. This time she would have paid anything to see Fiona and her baby. On returning to the bungalow she sent Tim to lie down and she sat in the living room, happily musing on pregnancies and babies, and how much joy and how much heartache they bring, sometimes all at the same time. Her own five boys were all out in the world, working, living away from home and content, as far as she knew. She recalled the teenage tantrums, the sibling rivalries and fights, and the rows that they caused between her and Richard, but would she have preferred not to have had them? Never. Her mind went back to Edna and her baby, her pregnancy without her husband, the birth and then the death of her little boy. Thinking of Joseph she burst into tears, prompting Tim to come in to find out what was wrong.

'Are you all right, sis?' he said.

'Yes, babies have that effect. They are so innocent and beautiful, and then it can go so wrong.'

'That's very depressing. What brought that on? Joseph is gorgeous; it's going to be perfectly OK.'

'Yes, I'm sorry Tim. Come on, you go and lie down and I'll make us some lunch. What've you got?'

'Food's in the cupboard there. You choose.'

'OK, I'll make a sandwich. Where's the bread?' asked Madeleine.

Tim pointed to the container on the work surface.

'The one that says BREAD on it!'

Madeleine made the lunch and she and Tim sat down to eat it in the kitchen. She decided not to mention the tale of little Paul, but she did say that she had been making some progress on the clock.

'What's the secret, then?' asked Tim.

'I haven't got that far yet, but I have spoken to one or two people who I am sure will be able to assist, and I have done some research on that business of the car going over the cliff.'

'The story the estate agents told?'

'Yes. I think there is a possibility that Stan, the driver of the car, might have survived. I cannot find any record of his death. Also his wife left the house a year or so afterwards, so they have both vanished. I think the clock is crucial in unravelling the mystery, but I am still trying to work out how it all fits in together. There was a piece in the paper four weeks after the event which said that Stan's body had not been found. Very odd.'

'Better not talk to Fiona about such things at the moment;' said Tim, 'she said the other day that she was concentrating on new lives not old ones. She has, however, kept Grace and Victoria in touch with her progress . I think they are both hoping to come this evening. I had a text from Grace saying that she and Perceval could come, and she thought that Victoria and Andy could as well. I'm waiting to hear on that.'

Madeleine was very pleased to learn that the girls and their boyfriends might visit. It would help them bond as a family, she thought, after all that had gone before. She had brought Tim home from the hospital which meant that his car was still parked there. She said she would take him back in this afternoon, say hello to Fiona and Joseph, and then make her way home. She thought Tim and Fiona would be better off on their own when bringing Joseph home for the first time. The worst thing, she knew from her own experience, was to have lots of people fussing around them.

They made their way back into the hospital at four o'clock to collect them. Walking into the ward Madeleine saw Fiona dressed and ready to leave, with tiny Joseph ready to meet the world. Fiona carried him carefully into the lift; she had been told not to use the stairs when carrying him, and Tim carried all the baby baggage that would form part of their lives for some time to come. With them safely ensconced in the car, Madeleine kissed them goodbye, and said she would come to help whenever required. She waved them off, with tears in her eyes.

Returning to The Haven seemed like moving into a different world, but her mind was still set on little Joseph and what he would make of the world.

Chapter Twenty

The days following Joseph's birth were busy ones for Madeleine, even though she was not nearby. She was in regular demand on the phone as Tim or Fiona rang to ask for advice, and she was also in touch with other members of the family, keeping them up to date with developments. She was enjoying having a new baby in the family, and travelled back to Emberton a couple of days after the birth, once Fiona was settled at home. Tim was still working part time at the planning office for the local council, but was on paternity leave and he and Fiona had asked Madeleine to stay with them for a few days, while they adjusted to being parents

It was, therefore, about ten days later when she saw Ian the next time. She had told him about Joseph, so he was not surprised when she was not in church the following Sunday. It was a week later, after church, that they had an opportunity to get together and chat about other things. Ian had not had the chance to fill Madeleine in with Jean Sanders' information concerning the receipt, and that she, Jean, thought that Lawrence and James was an expensive jewellers which may not have sold anything for as little as 19/11d. Madeleine was sceptical;

'Even expensive shops have some cheaper items,' she said, 'unless they are very grand, which I don't think would be the case in Seatown. My guess is that this receipt is for a ring. But what sort of ring, I wonder. Could have been an engagement ring for an engagement that did not lead to a wedding, I suppose. Or even a wedding ring, but then he didn't get married for many years. How old would Eric have been in 1952? When did Tina say he was born?'

'1919,' replied Ian. 'So he would have been thirty two or three. He didn't marry Tina's mum until he was in his late forties. Was he married before perhaps, and it was a memento of his first marriage?'

'But in that case we should be able to find him getting married. Maybe we should look for that. What else would the receipt be for? What else do jewellers sell?'

'Bracelets, brooches, watches, some clocks. The difficulty is knowing what price things would have been in 1952. It makes it very tricky to match the receipt with a purchase when you don't know how much everything was,' said Ian.

'Any more thoughts about the number in the envelope? Why would anyone keep a number on a bit of old paper? Why did Eric keep it? And why didn't Tina bin it when she found it in his stuff from the home? She must have felt it was important somehow.'

'I haven't any ideas on what it might be, apart from what we said last week. As far as why Tina kept it, perhaps she thought that if her dad had kept a bit of paper in an envelope then it must be important, so she would keep it as well.'

'Hmm, we're no further forward are we?' said Madeleine. 'But I did have one thought about our other puzzle. How old is Edna? On her marriage certificate she is nineteen, so she would be late seventies, maybe eighty now, if she's still alive.'

'Yes,' said Ian hesitantly, not quite sure where this was going.

'How old is Jean Sanders?'

'About that age, what are you suggesting?'

'I'm certainly not suggesting that Jean and Edna are one and the same person,' laughed Madeleine, 'no, but if she is about the same age, maybe she knew Edna, or something about what happened on that day.'

'Maybe, I suppose,' agreed Ian.

'You said that she had been associated with the church for many years. If she is Seatown born and bred, she would certainly know about the Haven Horror, and surely would also know something about the people involved.'

'But wouldn't she have said something before now. Presumably at the time there would have been lots of interest, and many people would have known something. Why did no one say anything? But then it was 1954; a different world. Maybe people kept themselves to themselves; didn't think it was any of their business. Anyway why don't we ask her?' suggested Ian.

'Was she in church this morning?'

'Yes, she's over there,' said Ian pointing to a stout woman with grey hair standing near the organ. 'Come on, I'll introduce you.'

Ian guided Madeleine through the crowd of coffee drinkers.

'Good morning Jean,' Ian said, brightly, 'have you met Madeleine? She's fairly new to the town.'

'No, I haven't. Hello Madeleine, I'm Jean Sanders. I polish the brass.'

'Hello Jean. It's very beautiful, it's so important to have a well cared for look in the church, isn't it?'

'Madeleine is the friend I was telling you about the other day when we were talking about Lawrence and James, the jewellers,' said Ian.

'I remember,' said Jean, 'beautiful shop. Such a shame.'

'Madeleine lives at The Haven,' said Ian.

Jean looked again at Madeleine.

'You know about what happened there then?' she asked.

'I think so,' replied Madeleine. 'I am interested to know about the woman who lived there though; Edna Proctor.'

Jean looked around.

'Come over here,' she said, rather furtively. She walked across to the other side of the church and sat down on one of the chairs.

'This all seems very secret,' said Madeleine.

'Just need to be a bit careful, that's all,' she said. 'Now, what did you want to know?'

'I wondered if you might have known her,' said Madeleine, 'I would guess that you would have been similar in age.'

Jean looked around again.

'Edna Fox, that's who she was, before she was married; she was two years older than me. But we were at the same school for a little time. In those days you left at fifteen, so when I was thirteen she would have left. I didn't know her very well because she was that bit older than me, but there were some things I knew about her.'

Madeleine was becoming more hopeful of a breakthrough, but Jean was determined to take her time.

'Pretty girl, she was. She knew it though; dark hair and dimples, very slim. When she left school she went to work at the baker's shop in town. Funnily enough it was next door to that jewellers, Lawrence and James. A few years later she married a bus driver, what was his name? Stan; that was it. We all thought it strange at the time, girl like her marrying a chap so much older. There were those who suggested she was in the family way, and that's why she married him. No baby arrived though, at least not then.'

'What happened to her, after the 'incident'?' asked Ian.

'The landslide was a five-minute wonder in the paper, I remember. He never came back,' said Jean.

Madeleine interrupted her flow;

'What do you mean, "he never came back"?'

'Well, they never found a body, did they? They always get washed up, sooner or later. He never did, so he must have survived and scarpered, for some reason.'

'Why would that have been?' persisted Madeleine.

'No idea. She spent some time in hospital afterwards, I remember that, and then she did have a baby, who died when he was tiny. I don't know any more after that. I do remember one thing, though. When she was at school she was always a popular girl, lots of boyfriends, you know the type. One of her admirers was a lad named John, lived over at Little Morton Farm. Should have stuck with him, shouldn't she?'

'Why?' asked Madeleine, 'why's that?'

'She'd have been rich. He's now John Williams, the founder and owner of PPS, the packaging company.'

Madeleine took a deep breath. Trying not to look too shocked, she said thank you to Jean, and turning to Ian suggested they left as soon as possible. Talking to the vicar near to the west door was a smart elderly man, whose eye Madeleine did not wish to catch.

Chapter Twenty One

Ian and Madeleine slipped out of the church by the south door, and as they walked down the path to the market place Madeleine said;

'You didn't tell me John Williams would be there. That could have got a bit embarrassing if he had overheard our conversation with Jean.'

'Sorry,' said Ian, 'he doesn't often come. He goes to the church in Steeple Morton and comes here occasionally, when there is no service there. Anyway what did we say about him?'

'Nothing really. Clearly Jean had seen him, and was feeling a little awkward. She's a bit of an odd one, isn't she? "I polish the brass", funny way to introduce yourself.'

'Yes, I think we're all used to her. An eccentric, but more interesting for that than a bunch of bland stereotypes.'

'Talking of eccentrics,' said Madeleine, 'who's the old boy who sits outside in the churchyard? I've seen him there each time I've come. He never speaks, just stares out at the traffic going by and occasionally writes something down.'

'Don't know much about him at all,' admitted Ian. 'His name's Alf, I think. He keeps himself very much to himself. He's rarely, if ever, in church.'

'Not a good match for Jean, then.' Madeleine chuckled at the thought. She brought herself back to reality.

'Ian, why don't you come back with me for some lunch? Nothing fancy I'm afraid, but we can plan our next move.'

Ian readily agreed, and they set off back to The Haven. The sun was shining and Madeleine rustled up a quick salad which they ate outside, savouring the view as well as the food.

'You are so lucky living here,' said Ian, 'I would love it. The sea air, the sunshine, no neighbours.'

'That sounds very unfriendly,' said Madeleine.

'You know what I mean. Here you can sit out in your own garden and have a conversation, without worrying that someone will overhear you; or that you will overhear them. It's a bit disconcerting when you can hear the clink of crockery and the rattle of cutlery through the hedge or over the fence.'

The lunch finished, Madeleine went back into the house to make a drink.

'Tea or coffee?' she called.

'Tea please,' came the reply.

As she waited for the kettle to boil she thought about the conversation with Jean. There was something she had said which rang a vague bell, but she was unable to put her finger on it. The more she thought about it, the less she could remember it. Maybe Ian would have an idea.

She carried the tray out into the garden. She had bought a small table and chairs for use outside which were proving invaluable in the good weather they had been having.

'Thanks,' said Ian, picking up his cup.

'While I was making the tea I was trying to remember something that Jean said which rang a bell, and I can't think what it was. Any ideas?'

'There was quite a lot she said. Interesting about Edna I thought. Puts a slightly different slant on things doesn't it?'

Madeleine sat quietly, gazing over the cliffs.

'I know what it was,' she said suddenly, 'but I don't know why it is important, or even if it's important. It was the address.'

'Madeleine, you've lost me. What are you talking about?'

'I said that something that Jean had said rang a bell, and it was the address.'

'Which address?'

'Jean said that John Williams, the boyfriend, lived at Little Morton Farm.'

'Yes; so what?'

'That's it. I don't know, but I am sure that it has cropped up before.'

'John Williams lives at Steeple Morton. That's what you're getting confused with.'

'No, it wasn't that. I had remembered that, but it was something else. Sounds as if he has gone up in the world anyway, from Little to Steeple,' insisted Madeleine.

'Some people may see it like that, but not everyone. Funny how villages across the country are like that. The Slaughters in the Cotswolds, the Snorings in Norfolk and the Stoweys in Somerset. The Mortons are the same here. Each village proudly independent of its neighbour.'

'Never mind where he lives or lived, is he significant?' asked Madeleine.

'I am not sure. Jean said that she had plenty of admirers. Pretty girl as she was it's not surprising. If he wasn't so high profile locally, you would think nothing of it. Just because he's rich and your landlord doesn't make him any more or less significant now.'

'I suppose,' said Madeleine, 'if she was that pretty, you wonder why she married a man thirteen years older than her, if she wasn't pregnant.'

'Maybe she liked more mature men. Jean said it was at school he was an admirer. If they left at fifteen and she married Stan at nineteen, what's John been doing all this time?'

'Admiring other girls. He was only a boy, Ian.'

The warm breeze coming in off the sea was ideal. They sat in companionable silence watching the seagulls swirl around the cliffs, and the small white horses dancing on the tops of the waves. Madeleine racked her brains about that address. All to no avail.

'So what about Eric?' asked Ian. 'Are you going to look him up and try to do the other bit you promised Tina?'

'Yes. I will do. When did Tina say he was born? I wrote it down somewhere, I'll go and check. Why don't you pour more tea while I go and look him up?'

Ian agreed and went into the house carrying the cups. Madeleine went into the dining room, where she kept her computer, and found the note she had made when Tina had visited. She found what she was looking for straightaway. It was twenty third of November 1919. She logged on and searched the indexes for the birth. The birth certificate will give me everything I need, she thought.

Keying in the details she waited for the results, and was taken aback to see that there were no births in Dorset of an Eric Smith in either 1919 or 1920. She called through to Ian;

'There isn't an Eric Smith born in Dorset at the right time. Maybe he was born elsewhere, but I would have thought that Tina would have said so. Shall I give her a ring?'

'Yes,' Ian replied, 'but I wouldn't say at the moment that you can't find her dad being born. Just ask if he was born in the county. If she says yes, we'll have another think.'

Madeleine made the phone call, and was not surprised when Tina confirmed that her dad had been born in Dorset. Madeleine thanked her, and said she would be in touch when she had news to impart.

'What are you going to do now?' asked Ian.

'I am going to order his marriage certificate. That will give me his father's name and occupation, and I may be able to trace his parents that way.'

She checked the date of the marriage, 1965, and found it easily. Eric Smith marrying Sylvia Harris in the third quarter of 1965.

'That's the one.'

A couple more clicks and she had placed the order for the marriage certificate.

Ian carried the cups of tea out into the garden, where the sun was still warm and the breeze pleasant. Madeleine started to tell Ian about Fiona and her new baby, but then stopped short, wondering if Ian, without that experience, wanted to hear anything about babies at all. She was pleased when he asked her to continue, and especially pleased when she could see he was enjoying her delight as much as she was. He really is a very nice man, she thought to herself.

Chapter Twenty Two

John Williams had seen Madeleine Porter in church that morning chatting to Jean Sanders. He had known Jean, or least known of her, for most of his life. He had known her as Jean Silverton at school in the late forties, when she had been in the same class as his friend Tony Birchwood. Tony was two years younger than him, but they had grown up together on neighbouring farms, and as such remained close until Tony's emigration with his family to New Zealand just after John had left school. They had always intended to keep in touch, and had done so for a while, but their lives then took different turns. He had been sad to learn that Tony had been killed in a sailing accident off South Island, New Zealand, when he was only twenty nine. That was many years ago now.

But Jean was still here in Seatown, almost a part of the furniture. She had been an unattractive girl, who had grown into an unattractive woman. No ugly duckling, he thought. He knew she had become very closely involved with the church when her husband had died, although she had been a regular attendee with him. Now she would proudly announce to anyone who cared to listen that she 'polished the brass'. He wondered if Madeleine was just getting the 'polish the brass' bit when he first saw them talking, but then he noticed her look across towards him, and guide Madeleine and Ian Clay away to the other side of the building.

John had seen Madeleine's advert in the parish magazine about researching family history, and he wondered whether that was the subject of their conversation, but he was concerned it was something more personal to him. He was going to try to get closer to find out, but the vicar greeted him, and started to talk to him about a fund-raising event in the offing. The next time John looked up, the little group had dispersed and Madeleine and Ian were gone.

He did not feel that he had any reason to be anxious about Madeleine meeting Jean, but he had a vague sense of unease, especially bearing in mind Madeleine's interest in personal family history research. He realised that sounded contradictory, but his own feelings about his past were also contradictory. He wondered whether he should speak to Madeleine, and perhaps ask her to do some work for him, and in that way he would know, or even perhaps control, what she could find out.

Of course there was the business of the Mary Treacy will. He did not know why he should be the beneficiary of this will when he was sure there was someone else who should have been. Perhaps he should ask Madeleine to look into it. Could he do that without her finding out other things, he wondered. It was a risk, but he was erring on the side of taking that risk. It was unfortunate for him that he had no one he could chew it over with first; there was Jeremiah Lewis, but he thought Jeremiah was a solicitor first and a friend second, and that was the wrong way round.

What about Ian Clay? Ian had worked for PPS for twenty years or more and John knew him to be a man of high integrity and honesty. Perhaps he could chat with him, and find out what Madeleine might do. He reached for the phone book and checked his number and then dialled.

'Ian Clay speaking,'

'Ian, it's John Williams. Sorry to trouble you. I wanted to ask you something which is a bit delicate. About some work. Can we meet for a drink perhaps, and I'll fill you in?'

'It's nice to hear from you,' replied Ian, 'but I'm not looking for any work at the moment; is it to do with the company? If so I'm rather out of touch.'

'Yes, of course. No, it was something more personal, but I would prefer to have a chat face-to-face. How about tomorrow lunchtime at the Fox and Grapes here in Steeple Morton? They do a good pint and the food's not bad.'

'I'm stewarding in the church tomorrow, but I can make Friday if you want to.'

Ian was pleased he had the excuse about the next day. He didn't want to appear too keen, but he was intrigued by the suggestion that he would be able to do personal work for John Williams. He must tell Madeleine before Friday.

'OK.' replied John, 'about twelve thirty? ... Good. I'll see you then.'

As soon as he had put the phone down Ian rang Madeleine and told her about the conversation with Williams. Both of them wondered if it was a follow-up to their chat with Jean at the weekend. Ian said that he would pop into The Haven on his way home from Steeple Morton on Friday afternoon to bring her up-to-date.

The Fox and Grapes in Steeple Morton was in keeping with the rest of the village; smart and expensive. The beer might be good, thought Ian as he walked in, but the prices were beyond him.

'Hello Ian, glad you could come.'

Ian had worked for John Williams' company for many years and Williams had been a good boss. However in Ian's experience he was not normally such a hail-fellow-well-met sort of person. It all seemed slightly false.

'What will you have?'

'Orange juice thank you,' said Ian, 'driving,'

'Have a look at the menu, on me. I'll get the drinks.'

Ian picked up the menu and decided that his view of the place as smart and expensive was spot on. Still he was not paying, so why not. When Williams returned with the drinks Ian ordered a fillet steak; John Williams did the same.

'Cheers, John,' said Ian raising his glass.

'Cheers.'

'While we are waiting,' said Ian, 'why not tell me what you want me to do?'

'I will. What I have to say is very personal, so I would want you to keep it confidential. I know that you have become friendly with Madeleine Porter, and I saw her advert in the parish magazine. I would have no objection to you sharing what I have to say with her, but no one else.'

'I understand.'

'I thought it might be easier to speak to you first because I know you better than I know her. Maybe you could tell me whether you and she would be able to do what I am going to ask you. Don't be afraid to say no if you don't want to, or can't, do it.'

'OK,' agreed Ian.

'A few weeks ago I had a telephone conversation with my solicitors, Hughes and Lewis, in Seatown. They told me that I was a beneficiary of a will; a sole beneficiary. As you will be aware, I am a wealthy man, so the amount of the legacy, though reasonable, is not sufficient for me to be affected by it, one way or the other. I am not reliant in any way on the amount I might inherit under the will. I was very surprised by this conversation, because although I knew the deceased, obviously, I would have put money on there being a close relative who would have been in line to benefit. I was not related to the deceased, either by blood or marriage.'

'So what do you want me, or us, to do?'

'I would like you to find the person whom I think should inherit this money. I will pay you the going rate, plus your expenses. I would like you to report to me weekly with your progress, and I will decide when and if you have done enough; unless, of course, you are successful, and find the person concerned.'

'That sounds reasonable,' said Ian. 'You must understand that when I talk to Madeleine, Mrs Porter, she may not want to do this, and then it would all be off.'

'Yes. Now let me tell you the details. The deceased is a Mary Treacy, and I believe she had a child, and it is that child whom I think should inherit.'

'What is the child's name?'

'I don't know. I think it was a boy, but I'm not sure. The child was born in 1955, that's all I can tell you.'

'It's not very much,' said Ian, 'Treacy quite a good name to research, though. Good job it wasn't Williams.'

Offended, John Williams looked at Ian, but said nothing. Then the food arrived and the meal was eaten in an atmosphere of mutual misunderstanding. Small talk filled the uncomfortable silences, but Ian was cross with himself for making a remark that was so easily misinterpreted. However, the steak was excellent, as was the rest of the meal. Ian thanked John, and said he or Madeleine would ring as soon as they had had chance to consider the offer.

As arranged Ian called in at The Haven on his way back from Steeple Morton. Madeleine welcomed him in and he had barely sat down before he was telling her about John Williams' curious assignment.

'Why ask me, and not you direct? I don't know. He said it was because he knew me better than he knew you, but I thought there was more to it than that, I don't know what. Anyway he said I could involve you in the search. He wants us to trace the child, who he thinks was a boy, of a Mary Treacy who died recently. Apparently Williams is the sole beneficiary under her will, but he clearly thinks her child should benefit.'

'That makes sense,' said Madeleine, 'it's what you would expect. Who is Mary Treacy and why does he think she had a child? Why isn't he sure of the sex of the child? Makes no sense.'

'He didn't say, except that he thought it might have been a boy. The only thing he did say for certain was that the child was born in 1955, but he didn't say where.'

'That's not a lot of help. Are you sure he didn't say any more?'

'Yes, I am. I did rather put my foot in it, which may have prevented him saying more.'

'Oh dear, what did you do?'

'It wasn't what I did, it was what I said. When he said the name was Treacy and told me very little else, I said it was a good name to research, meaning because it was an unusual name, and then I said it was a good job it wasn't Williams. I only meant that Williams was a common name, and with limited information it might have been difficult, but I think he thought I was suggesting he was the father of the child, and he shut up then.'

'Was this Mary Treacy married, did he say?'

'I don't know. Oh dear, I don't think I have done very well.'

'Never mind,' consoled Madeleine, 'we'll see what we can find. I'm not hopeful at all. As a start let's assume that the child was born locally, then if that produces nothing we will widen the search. Even if we find someone, how do we know it's the right person? He would know, I suppose.'

'Before you do anything, should you ring him and say you will do it?'

'Good idea,' said Madeleine, 'I'll do that immediately, while you put the kettle on.'

Ian obeyed his orders, and while he was in the kitchen he heard Madeleine on the phone, confirming that she would do what she could, and report back to him with progress. He made the tea and carried it through to Madeleine.

'I couldn't get any more out of him,' she said, 'so I told him I thought it was a needle in a haystack job, but he wanted me to carry on. I apologised on your behalf, and he apologised in return for having misunderstood you.'

She fetched the laptop and started to search.

'Anyone named Treacy born in 1955, let's have a look.'

'Here we are, twenty names, none of them in Dorset, though. Not much help, is it?' None of them even close. I wonder why he thought she had had a child.'

'What about Mary herself. If she was not married we should be able to find her birth,' suggested Ian, 'try that.'

Madeleine tried but to no avail. There were a number of Mary Treacys, but again none of them born in Dorset.

'No one in Dorset, but did he say she was born locally? One last chance,' said Madeleine, 'if she was married we should be able to find a man named Treacy marrying someone called Mary.'

She paused.

'No, just as bad. No Treacy marrying a Mary in Dorset at any time, and only a few anywhere at the right time. Mr Williams is going to have to give us more information if he wants to make serious progress. Without knowing dates and places there really is nothing else we can do. I'll let him know.'

She rang him again and told him the disappointing news. He was hesitant about giving her further information, so she left the matter with him to contact her if he wanted to proceed. Putting the phone down, she said to Ian, irritably;

'He knows more, but isn't telling us. Why not? He either wants to find this person or not. And if he does why did he ask us to look with such limited information?'

Chapter Twenty Three

Madeleine was now busy on a number of fronts. She was still helping Fiona with the occasional 'new mum' question, she was researching Tina's grandparents, she was puzzling over Mary Treacy's child and the cuckoo clock remained an enigma.

In addition to this were the two bits of paper given to her by Tina, the receipt and the number. She was confident she had more or less resolved the receipt question. She knew the type of shop and could make a guess at what it was for, but the number remained out of reach. She was awaiting the arrival of Eric Smith's marriage certificate, but guessing that the receipt was for a ring, wedding or engagement, she decided to search for a previous marriage for Eric Smith. There were three possibilities, but none of them seemed likely contenders, some having other names, which Madeleine was sure Eric did not have, and others getting married on the other side of the county. She realised that that did not preclude it being the right person, but it did not seem likely.

She thought back to her other enquiries. She had been unable to find a birth for Eric Smith, or a marriage which would accord with the receipt. She had been similarly unsuccessful in her search for Mary Treacy being born, getting married or having a child. Then there was the tale told by Jean Sanders about John Williams being sweet on Edna Fox. She wondered if she was being unlucky or unskilful in her searches. She wished she could remember why that address of John Williams sounded vaguely familiar.

Ian was on stewarding duty today so she could not share her thoughts with him. She was beginning to miss seeing him on his 'work' days. She put her thoughts to one side as she determined to sort out and tidy up the mess in the loft and the barn. It would be useful if she were to stay on for the winter to have outside storage space, and most of it at present was taken up with old junk. She always dressed casually, but in view of the task ahead she put on a scruffy jumper and old jeans, and was about to embark on her project when she heard the postman. She hesitated, then went to the front door and saw an envelope which she knew would contain Eric's marriage certificate.

Sitting down in the kitchen she opened it, and looking at the details, there was nothing unexpected: on July 18 1965, at St Martin's Church, Seatown, between Eric Smith, age 45, bachelor, of 39 Harold Street, Seatown, driver, to Sylvia Jennifer Harris age 24, spinster, of 11, Victoria Street, Seatown, clerk. Eric's father's name was given as Jonathan Smith, agricultural labourer, deceased, and Sylvia's as Alexander Harris, fisherman.

Madeleine noticed that he was a bachelor so it was not surprising she had been unable to find a previous marriage. Perhaps the jeweller's shop receipt was not for a ring, after all. Although it was what she had expected, it was not what she had hoped for. She was hoping that there would be some clue which would help her with the receipt and the number. There appeared not to be. However Tina had asked Madeleine to trace her grandparents and as far as

Eric was concerned she knew that, being born in 1919, his father would be on the 1911 census. That would be easy, she thought. A quick look at the census showed that was not the case. There was no Jonathan Smith living in Dorset at the time of that census. Madeleine was becoming more and more frustrated. Everything she looked up was not there. She did not question her own abilities; she was coming to the conclusion that someone, and maybe more than one person, was not telling the truth, or at least not the whole truth.

She rang Tina and suggested that she should come over to talk about Eric that evening. They arranged their meeting for eight o-clock, then Madeleine texted Ian to tell him that Tina was coming, and would he like to come earlier for a bite to eat and an up-date. She swiftly received an answer in the affirmative.

In between trying to eat spaghetti bolognaise without making too much mess. Madeleine explained what had happened about Eric. Ian agreed that it seemed that there were some discrepancies and that Tina, like John Williams, should be encouraged to tell the complete story if they wanted Madeleine to find the answers to their respective problems.

Tina arrived a few minutes late, on her own. Kevin had a meeting in town and had dropped her off beforehand. He had told Tina that he would pick her up later if she let him know what time to collect her. Once again she took her shoes off at the door, but she seemed more relaxed than she had been on her previous visit.

Madeleine started with the positive news.

'I bought a copy of your dad's marriage certificate so that I could find the name of his father,' she said. 'I see that when he was married he was living at Harold Street in Seatown. Is that where you were born?'

'Yes, well, in hospital, but that's where Mum and Dad were living at the time. I remember Harold Street. It was in the older part of the town, built before the war. Terraced it was, but cosy. I liked it there.'

Tina perked up, reliving her childhood memories of living and playing at Harold Street. She said how she started school while they were living there, and recalled the short walk across the town to St Saviour's Infants School.

'How long had your Dad lived there before he was married, do you know?' asked Ian.

'I'm not sure. I never heard him talk about anywhere else, so I guess it must have been a long time.'

'And he worked as a driver, it says,' said Madeleine, 'had he always been a driver?'

'Yes, drove different things all his life. I think he was a driver in the war as well. Don't know who with, but he did sometimes say about driving lorries and buses for the soldiers. Sorry I can't be of any more help.'

'That's OK,' said Madeleine, 'You know I asked you if he was born in Dorset, when I phoned?'

'Yes'

'That was because I couldn't find any record of his birth. All births are registered in the town or district they occur in. If your dad was born in Dorset, it would say so in the registers. I need to find his birth certificate to find his mother's name. Did he ever mention his mum?'

'I can't remember that he did. Like I said he was never one to talk much. Maybe he just got missed off the register for some reason. Must happen.'

Madeleine was reluctant to say that it was very rare for such a thing to happen. She tried a different tack.

'Your Mum's dad was a fisherman, I see. Did you have much to do with those grandparents?'

'No. Like I said Mum and Dad didn't get on very well. Dad didn't like Mum's dad. Said he was interfering. They lived along the coast at Brixham, but we saw very little of them, then nothing after the divorce. When Dad was ill, these last few years, I would go and see him and talk to him. I never knew if he even realised I was there but I chatted to him, told him about things, how Jimmy was getting on, where he'd been. Sometimes he would say ''hello darling'' and I am sure he thought it was someone else. Don't know who, though. He never called Mum ''darling''; not that I ever heard. Then he'd say ''you don't deserve it'', and get very cross. I would call the nurse when that happened, and they would calm him down.'

'Did that happen often?' asked Madeleine.

'A few times. Don't know what brought it on. Maybe it was something I said, who knows?'

'Did he say anything else?' enquired Ian, hoping for some insight into what he was thinking.

'Just the odd ramble about cricket. He was a great fan. He'd talk about players I'd never heard of. Nothing else.'

'Tina, we're struggling here to get anywhere. What I am going to do is to have a look at the electoral register for Harold Street in 1965 when your dad was living there. If I work backwards from there I will be able to find when he moved in. That might help,' said Madeleine.

'Do I owe you any money? Have I had my free hour?'

'Yes, you have, but I've got so interested in this case I'll carry on for the time being for free. I bought the marriage certificate which was £9.25 which you can have if you want to.'

'Thanks, I'll pay you for that.'

She took a ten pound note out of her purse and gave it to Madeleine.

'Don't worry about the change as you're carrying on. By the way, what happened about the receipt and number?'

'Oh, I'd nearly forgotten that. Lawrence and James was a jeweller's shop which closed in the late sixties. Apparently very expensive. If the receipt was for a ring it wasn't a wedding ring because he didn't marry until your mum in 1965, so I don't know. There's nothing else to indicate what it might have been for. Could have been a brooch or earrings, or maybe a watch for himself. The number is still a puzzle though; leave it with me.'

She handed the shop receipt, which she had copied for future reference if necessary, back to Tina.

'Thanks,' said Tina, 'you've been very helpful. I'd better be off. I'll text Kevin and ask him to fetch me.'

Madeleine made a drink for them all while they awaited Kevin's arrival. It was not going at all well. After Tina had gone home, she told Ian how she had been going to sort out the barn that morning, but had been distracted by the arrival of the postman with Eric Smith's marriage certificate. As she was telling him her mind returned to that address, but, annoyingly, it would still not come to her where she had seen it before.

On their way home Tina told Kevin what Madeleine had found.

'It's funny doing this after Dad's died,' she said, 'I wish I'd asked him things before. I know so little about him before he married Mum, and now Mrs Porter says she can't find his birth certificate. Doesn't that seem odd to you?'

'Don't worry so, she's all right is Madeleine. She'll sort it out.'

'I know, but I seem a bit lost without him. Silly really; we weren't that close, but now he's gone, it's difficult.'

She sniffed a tear away.

'I sometimes wonder if he could hear any of what I used to talk to him about. I would tell him about Jimmy and where he'd been, and you, and how good you are to me.'

She smiled and cried all at the same time.

'Get me home and cheer me up, Kevin.'

He patted her leg gently.

'OK.'

Chapter Twenty Four

John Williams was cross. He was cross with himself. It was more than that, he was infuriated with himself. He had invited Ian Clay for a chat about a small project that he wanted him to take on with his friend Madeleine Porter, and he let himself be irritated by a slip of the tongue. He knew Clay well enough to know that he would not have made such an inference, and yet he had let that slip upset him. Then, when Madeleine Porter had phoned and told him she had been unable to find what he had asked her to look for, he had refused to give her any further information. That was stupid. And why was he being so stupid, he asked himself? Because he was feeling vulnerable. Mary Treacy's death and the benefit coming to him under her will had upset his equilibrium. He was a man who had been the boss for so many years; it was difficult for him to be subject to someone else, especially when that someone else was beyond his power to control.

He did not know for certain the place of birth of Mary's child, but he did know the gender, and he was certain of the date because she had told him. It was so many years ago now, but he remembered the letter. Everything was so different now, it would be more open and above board. But it was too late now. If only he hadn't had to go abroad for all that time. Then there was that notice in the paper; that had been the cause of the trouble originally. It would all have been different if they, whoever they were, had not got that wrong.

He drifted off into his imagination. Marrying her, settling down, having a family. Someone to pass the business on to, with a bit of luck. After she had gone he had devoted his life to the business, and had made a great success of it. Maybe, if things had been different, he would not have been able to build it up the way he had.

He might be a great-grandfather now, with energetic boys and pretty little girls running rings around him, and he would be loving it.

'Tell me about when you were young, G-G,' they would say, 'was Great Granny pretty?'

'She was beautiful,' he would reply, 'and still is.'

She would look across the room at him, those dimples now formed into small creases under her eyes. The door on the clock would open and the cuckoo would appear to tell the time. The children would shriek for joy and wait, excitedly, for the next time.

Tears started to roll down his cheeks as he sat in his beautiful house, regretting all the mistakes of the past, both his own and other people's, wishing that things had been done differently. He started to give serious thought to how he could improve the situation. Perhaps a phone call to Madeleine Porter would be a good place to start.

Chapter Twenty Five

'Ian, I've remembered,' she said excitedly.

Madeleine and Ian were enjoying the afternoon sun in the garden at the Haven. She was very pleased that she had met someone with whom she was able to share her investigations and discoveries, and whom she found very comfortable to be with. The question of the address had been nagging at her for days; she was convinced she had come across it somewhere else, and had not been able to bring it to mind. Suddenly all was clear, and she sat bolt upright in her chair.

'Remembered what?' asked Ian.

'The address. I said to you that the address Jean Sanders mentioned where John Williams lived was familiar.'

'Yes, and I said it was because it was Steeple Morton not Little Morton.'

'But it is Little Morton that I recall seeing. It was a while ago, when Fiona and Tim were here we were exploring the house, and Tim went up into the attic. There was a load of old furniture and general junk up there. Anyway he found a staircase that went down from the attic straight into the old barn at the side of the house. So he came down from the attic and all three of us went into the barn, which was full of similar junk. Let me show you.'

She grabbed his hand and pulled him round to the barn.

'In here,' she said, opening the rickety door. See that table over there, have a look at the box on top of it.'

Ian reached over to the table and picked up the box, which was very grubby. He coughed as the dust from the table flew up.

'Bring it outside.'

Madeleine went into the kitchen and emerged with a bright yellow cloth. Ian put the box on the stone path and Madeleine wiped the duster across it. There was the address; John Williams, Little Morton Farm, Seatown.

'So what?' asked Ian, 'when he was doing up the place he brought something in a cardboard box which had originally been sent to him.'

'But he lives at Steeple Morton, doesn't he? How long ago was it that he lived at Little Morton? If it was just to transport bits and pieces here, why not throw the box away when you have done so. It looks in a pretty poor state of repair anyway. He must have had something sent to him in this box when he lived at Little Morton Farm; that seems obvious, but why keep it?'

Madeleine leaned over and lifted the box lid. Inside were some screwed up sheets of newspaper which had been used to cushion whatever the contents had been. She looked round and Ian had gone. A few moments later he came out of the front door, gently carrying the cuckoo clock.

'Careful!' shouted Madeleine.

Ian carefully put the clock into the box. It fitted into the shape made by the newspaper.

'There,' he said triumphantly. 'That's what was in the box.'

Madeleine was looking down at the clock, bewildered.

'I think we should put it back. What if it has stopped working?'

'Don't fret, it'll be OK.'

Ian lifted the clock out and just as carefully as he had carried it out, carried it back into the living room, and replaced it on the wall. He listened, and was relieved to hear it ticking.

'Perfectly OK,' he said, keeping his fingers crossed.

'That's only part of the problem, though,' said Madeleine, still shaking after seeing Ian manoeuvre the clock in and out of the box.

'Who sent it to him? And when and why?' she continued. 'I wonder if Jean Sanders would know when he left Little Morton Farm. That would give us a clue as to when it might have been sent.'

'Do you want to involve her any more in this? John Williams seemed a bit wary about involving anyone else in the case of Mary Treacy. He probably wouldn't take kindly towards us talking to anyone about his precious clock either,' counselled Ian.

'You're right. We'll have to think again. Now I've cleaned it off, bring the box in and let's have another look at it. I know it's very old but is there a postmark?'

Ian brought the box into the kitchen and put it on the table. The writing of the address was very faint, and there were stamps on the box in pre-decimal currency, but there was no legible postmark.

'Can't read it,' he said, 'not surprising. Stamps don't really help, except that it was pre 1971. Do you think that is a woman's writing?'

'Difficult to say, isn't it. On balance I would say yes. It's slightly more rounded than a man's might be. I'm no expert though, so I wouldn't bank on it.

They sat in silence in the kitchen, trying to work out who might have sent the clock to John Williams and when.

'There's nothing to say where it was posted, so he might have bought it through a newspaper and had it posted to him. That would account for a woman's writing on the box, if indeed it is, if she were a worker in the despatch department of a large shop,' said Madeleine.

'I think you're right. That seems the most likely explanation. I wonder what sort of shop was selling mail order in the fifties and sixties.'

'Lots, I should think,' said Madeleine, 'I remember my mum buying loads by mail order when we were growing up; clothes, shoes, general household things. Sometimes she seemed to buy more by post than going out to the town shops.'

'That's not a lot of help, is it?' said Ian, 'if Williams bought it mail order, then why is it such a treasured possession that he would spend thousands of pounds to house it? Crazy!'

'What's the alternative?'

'Think about it this way,' said Ian, 'forget that it is a clock for the minute. Imagine you have a much valued possession which you want to keep safe. Why would it be so treasured? Not because you bought it mail order, surely.'

'Why can't a mail order purchase become a treasured possession?' interrupted Madeleine.

'There's too much chance involved. If you value it so much you would have been very careful when buying it. Unless, of course, you didn't buy it at all. If a loved one gave it to you, then it would become special, especially if that loved one was far away, or not around any more. Look at my watch.'

Ian held out his arm and pushed up his sleeve.

'Janice gave this to me for our first wedding anniversary. It's probably not valuable, but to me it's priceless. If I'd bought it mail order it would be just a watch, if she bought it mail order and gave it to me, then it becomes something quite different.'

'So what you're saying is that someone very dear to John Williams bought this clock for him and gave it to him, thereby making it special.'

'Possibly.'

'Why only possibly? I thought that was what you said.'

'It is also possible,' said Ian,' that it was owned by someone else who then gave the clock to him as a gift. In the same way as my watch, the giving of it would make it valued.'

'So which is it, mail order purchase by Williams or a gift from a lover?' asked Madeleine.

'I don't think it has to be a lover, necessarily. It might be his mother or grandmother. It might be a family heirloom.'

'I'm just too romantic,' said Madeleine, 'I have a picture of this besotted young woman sending her beau a cuckoo clock.'

She laughed out loud.

'Oh dear, that doesn't sound very romantic at all, does it?' she added.

Ian returned to practicalities.

'It would help if we knew when it was sent.'

'Newspapers,' said Madeleine suddenly.

'Finding an advert for clocks in old newspapers is going to be a hard job, we wouldn't know if...'

'No, silly!' chipped in Madeleine. 'The box is full of newspapers which protected the clock. If they were the original packaging then we would have the date the clock was packed, and therefore sent.'

Madeleine pulled out the papers from the box on the table. They had been screwed up and some were torn. She pulled out one piece with a headline; ''heartthrob dies in car crash''. She flattened out the paper, which unfortunately was torn where the date would have been. It was a copy of the *Daily Mirror*. She read the article which detailed the death in a car crash of James Dean, the Hollywood star who died, according to the article, at the age of twenty four.

'When did James Dean die, it was the fifties wasn't it?' she asked Ian.

'Yes, I think so. He only made three films, didn't he? One of those who was set for great things,' said Ian. 'Bit like Achilles in Homer, who chose to die young and be remembered for ever, rather than dying old in obscurity.'

'I don't suppose for one moment that James Dean chose to die young,' said Madeleine. 'Anyway, when did he die? Google it.'

Ian discovered that James Dean's death occurred on 30 September 1955, and so the paper was probably the edition from 1 October.

'Goodness me,' exclaimed Madeleine, 'that is not long before Edna's little Paul died. So what is the connection between Paul and the clock? Or am I being too fanciful?'

'If you are not being fanciful, that means there is a connection between John Williams, the clock, Paul Proctor and Edna. A few weeks before Paul's death John Williams receives in the post a cuckoo clock sent to him in a box with a woman's handwriting on. Why? Is that Edna's hand? We don't know.'

'Jean Sanders said that John Williams was an admirer of Edna Fox. Maybe he was more than that. By the time the clock was sent, Stan has disappeared, whether dead or not, and Edna is living alone at The Haven. Maybe John and Edna got together.'

'Madeleine, we're talking the mid-fifties. People didn't 'get together', they got married. Any suggestion of John Williams moving in on a young widow, maybe not even that, would be frowned on most severely.'

'It could be coincidence,' said Madeleine, unenthusiastically. 'Bit difficult to ask him outright after our last encounter.'

'Indeed; perhaps he will come back to us with more information about the child he is looking for, and we can worm something more out of him. We will have to wait and see.'

Madeleine put the paper back into the box and returned it to the barn, when she noticed again the damaged furniture and utensils which had been kept. What further secrets might these hold, she wondered.

Walking back into the house she said to Ian;

'What are you doing tomorrow?'

'Sounds like an invitation to a date,' he chuckled, 'why?'

'I was thinking more of Dorchester Record Office and electoral registers, but we could do lunch again like before.'

'Oh, Eric, of course. With all the excitement of the clock box I had almost forgotten about poor Eric. Yes, I'm up for that. Will you pick me up?'

'A pleasure,' smiled Madeleine.

Chapter Twenty Six

Madeleine collected Ian the following morning as arranged and they drove into Dorchester to go to the record office. Unfortunately they were unable to find a space in the car park there, and had to park in one of the town's multi-stories. Walking downstairs towards the street, Madeleine's mind went back to their discoveries of the previous evening. She was still struggling to prove whether there was a connection between the clock being sent to John Williams and the death of Edna's baby soon afterwards. Did he know about Edna's pregnancy? Was he the father of the baby? She knew that Edna had put Stan as the father on the birth certificate, but as a married woman she would have done, whoever the father was. Despite turning it over and over in her mind she had been unable to discover a link between John Williams and Edna Proctor at that time. She knew from Jean Sanders that he had been an admirer at school, but that meant nothing, so were lots of other boys, no doubt. She was quickly coming to the conclusion that there was no link, and she was just making it up to suit her own theories.

'I give up,' she announced to Ian as they crossed the road to the Record Centre.

'Does that mean we're going home?'

'No, I'm giving up on the clock, Paul and John Williams, at least until he gets in touch again.

'Now, what about Eric Smith?

Ian and Madeleine signed in at the desk and sat down with the electoral registers they had requested. The main purpose of their visit was to find out how long Eric had lived at 65, Harold Street, which had been his home at the time of his marriage to Sylvia. But Madeleine had in mind that, as she had been unable to trace Eric's parents, she might have a poke around to see if she could make any progress on that as well. Being more used to the layout of the registers this time they found Harold Street in Seatown easily. Eric Smith was listed there in 1965, the register having been completed in the previous October, before he was married. Moving forwards they found Eric and Sylvia there in the following year's book, and then further onwards in subsequent volumes. As Tina had said, they lived at that address for quite some years.

Madeleine was now wanting to work backwards, to see how long Eric had been there before his marriage, and to see if there were any other occupants of the house during his time there. Her search was successful, finding Eric in 1964, 1963 and 1962.

'Looks as if he was in this house for a long time,' she said to Ian, 'Richard and I never stayed anywhere very long, certainly not ten years. He kept moving from parish to parish. It was very unsettling for the boys, especially with schooling.'

Madeleine looked up and saw the stern faces of other researchers glaring at her, presumably for talking too loudly. She mumbled an apology and returned to her search. She picked up 1961 and flicked through the pages until she found Harold Street. There it was, number 65, Eric Smith and Doreen Proctor.

'Ian, look,' she shouted, then, realising what she had done, glanced around the room apologetically.

'Let's go outside,' said Ian.

She put away her notebook and pencil, shrugged on her coat and walked out through the door. When she was outside she couldn't help herself;

'Who is she? Who is Doreen Proctor?'

'Calm down, let's think. How common is Proctor as a name locally? Maybe it was a lady friend, or a lodger. Granny? Aunt?'

'Unlikely to be a lady friend. As we said, they got married in those days. It's 1961, I don't think free love had reached Dorset by then. So who is she?'

'I don't think we can find that out at the moment; maybe when you get home,' replied Ian. 'In the meantime we need to continue looking for Eric, to see when he first came on the scene at Harold Street.'

They went back inside with apologies and promises of better behaviour, and continued their search. Eric and Doreen were also listed in the register for 1960, but going back to 1959, Madeleine found only Doreen Proctor listed as a voter.

'It looks as if Eric turned up in 1959 from somewhere. I wonder where from. I would guess that Doreen was the tenant, and she sublet to Eric. If she died, then Eric may have been able to take on the tenancy. Can we check if Doreen died or was married?'

'I think so, I'll go and ask,' said Ian.

Ian returned to Madeleine and explained how they would be able to buy the death certificate from Seatown Register Office today, but at a cost of £25. Although they both felt this a bit on the pricy side, they agreed to do so.

Arriving back in Seatown they located the Register Office and ordered the certificate, saying they would like it the same day. After a short delay the clerk returned with the document. They took it outside and sat down to take in the contents.

Date of death 26 June1961, at 65, Harold Street Seatown, Doreen Proctor, age 40, landlady, cause of death leukaemia, informant Eric Smith, driver, of 65 Harold Street.

'That doesn't tell us much. He was her tenant and found her dead, perhaps, so he registered the death.'

Ian sat in thought.

'Have you got a copy of Stan Proctor's birth certificate?' he asked.

'No, I didn't see the need. They're not cheap at £9.25.'

'I think you should buy Stan and Doreen's birth certificates. I reckon that they are brother and sister.'

'How does that help?' asked Madeleine.

'Tina said that her dad was born on 23 November 1919. On Stan Proctor's marriage certificate his age, in 1952, was thirty two. The same. You couldn't find Eric Smith's birth certificate because there isn't one. I think that Eric Smith and Stan Proctor are one and the same man. Let's go and buy the birth certificates, and then we need to check the details on Eric's and Stan's marriage certificates as well.'

Madeleine went back to the desk and ordered the two birth certificates, which, she was told, would be available in a week's time. She had already paid the priority price for Doreen's death certificate, and decided that she could wait for the others.

'We'll come back in a week,' he said, 'then I can be proved right.'

On arriving back at The Haven, and after the production of the requisite tea and biscuits, Madeleine laid out the marriage certificates of Stan Proctor and Eric Smith.

'Look at these; the ages are the same, given the difference in the date of the marriage, his occupation is very similar, driver and bus driver, fathers' names are interesting.'

'Why's that? They're different,' said Ian.

'Obviously the surname has to be the same as his own, but Smith is not very imaginative, is it? But look at the Christian names. Do you remember that Tina said her father loved reading Old Testament stories aloud? Do you recall which she said was his favourite?'

'No, I can't say that I do.'

'Well, I can. It was the story of David and Jonathan. Now look at the certificates. He has changed his father's name from David Proctor to Jonathan Smith. I think that clinches it.'

'Better not say anything to Tina for the moment. Let's wait for the birth certificates to confirm our suspicions,' said Ian.

'You realise what this means for Tina, I'm sure. It makes her father a bigamist, so his marriage to Sylvia Harris is invalid, which makes her illegitimate,' said Madeleine.

'Not necessarily,' said Ian, 'he might have divorced Edna or she might be dead.'

'In that case,' replied Madeleine, 'he wouldn't have needed to change his name, if indeed he did.'

'In any event, it doesn't count for much these days, but Tina might mind. When those birth certificates come we'll have another chat with her; better make sure that Kevin is with her this time. Don't want her getting upset.'

It was a few days later that the birth certificates came. When Madeleine read them she thought to herself that it was going to be a difficult conversation with Tina and Kevin. As she had predicted, Stan and Doreen were brother and sister, and therefore it seemed that Stan had metamorphosed into Eric at some point. That raised other questions, why, when and where, to start with.

She decided to speak to Ian first, and he called in to see her after his stint at the church.

'I hope you're staying for a bite, I've put together a salad,' she said to him.

'Sounds good, thanks,' Ian replied.

'So what is your theory?' he continued.

Madeleine settled back in the armchair and gazed around the room, trying to imagine it as it would have been when Stan was living here. The old furniture they had found up the attic and in the barn would be in here, nothing like their replacements. But, in all likelihood, one thing would be the same; the cuckoo clock, although she still didn't understand how that fitted into this story.

'This is what I think happened,' she said. 'Stan drives off that afternoon, don't know why, and is hit by a landslip. Somehow he survives the fall and goes off somewhere. Why doesn't he return? Presumably he doesn't want to, but I reckon that he didn't know that Edna was pregnant.'

'Because if he did, he would have returned?' asked Ian.

'Yes, I expect so. But then, if he knew it wasn't his; that would be a reason for not coming back.'

'We can't really know. Anyway what happens next?'

'Stan goes away and starts a new life. After a few years he comes back to Seatown and marries Sylvia, having changed his name to Eric Smith. He and Sylvia have a little girl. Then they get divorced, and she leaves.'

'Why would he return? Wouldn't someone recognise him?' pressed Ian.

'We don't know what was happening elsewhere which might have prompted him to come back. As far as being recognised, maybe he grew a beard, or shaved off his beard, wore glasses, I don't know. What I do know is that in the late fifties and early sixties there was not the interchange of information there is now. I think it would be easier to be anonymous. Also his sister might have been ill. Maybe he came home to look after her. She died of leukaemia a couple of years after his return.'

'And in exchange for that, Doreen kept her brother's secret. But wouldn't people put two and two together and realise it was her brother who was looking after her?' queried Ian.

'Stan Proctor had been killed in the Haven Horror incident. Doreen Proctor takes in a lodger, who doesn't look like her brother, who cares for her. What's wrong with that?'

'Hmm, I'm not sure. Anyway, whatever the reasoning behind it all, it seems as if Stan did return, take on a new name and marry Sylvia,' agreed Ian.

'In that case, would he have to do it by deed poll? The new name, I mean. If so, where's the documentation for that?'

'I am fairly sure you can change your name by saying that you want to be known by a new name. The difficulties arise with officialdom. I am only guessing, but I suspect that the taxman would want something official in writing; otherwise it might seem like an attempt to evade tax. Same for the NHS, and the Bank. Anything vaguely official you would have to produce a form for,' said Ian.

'So where is it? And who drew it up?' asked Madeleine.

'These days you can download a form, but in those days it would be a job for a solicitor. Maybe Tina would know if her dad ever had dealings with any of the town's solicitors.'

'Depends when he changed his name. Before he came back or after?'

'No need to before his return, but when he realised he was going to have to come back, he would have got it done as soon as possible. That could have been where he was living or here.   Who were the local solicitors in 1959/60?'

'Hold on,' said Madeleine, 'one step at a time. We ought to give Tina a ring and ask her to come and see me. We will sort out the question of the change of name later.'

They finished their salad and quite independently had the same thought;

'What about the clock?' they said together, and laughed.

'Great minds,' said Ian.

'If Stan survives the fall, and eventually returns to Seatown, does that have any bearing on the story of the clock and John Williams?' asked Madeleine.

'As far as we know, he never had any further contact with this house, Edna or the clock,' said Ian.

'No, you're right... I must ring Tina.'

Madeleine   busied   herself   with   making arrangements with Tina for her to come with Kevin. Tina needed to check with Kevin which days were suitable, and eventually they agreed a date. Meanwhile Ian stacked the dishwasher and made a drink. No more was said of the matter as they enjoyed each other's company for the evening.

Chapter Twenty Seven

He opened his eyes painfully and felt a cold liquid running down his face. He tried to touch his face with his hand but a pain shot through his shoulder and arm. He turned very carefully to look out of the window. The rain was lashing the back window of the car. Stan Proctor realised that he was alive, but in danger. The car was on its side on a flat rock ten feet above the crashing waves. The pain in his shoulder and arm made it difficult to move, but he knew that if he did not move, the car would soon slide off the rock, on to the more jagged rocks beneath and into the waves. Then it would be all over. Blood was running down his face from a cut above his eyes where he had fallen against the side of the car as it fell. The impact had damaged his right arm and shoulder and he was struggling to sit so that he could reach up to the other door, in order to get out.

His head hurt and he was having difficulty remembering what had happened. All he knew at that moment was that getting out of the car was more important than anything else. The wind was strong and the rain was pounding down. The car would not stay where it was for long. He reached out with his left hand and tried to grab the other door handle, to pull himself upwards, but it was out of reach. Fortunately his legs, apart from some bruising, were not hurt, and he was able to stand and reach towards the door.

He must get out, but he did not know what he would do when he had done so. First things first, he thought, as he pushed upwards on the passenger door. Immediately it was caught by the wind and slammed shut. He tried again and this time managed to hold the door against the wind. He put his feet on the seats, climbed out and crouched on the rock, the rain still soaking his thin clothing. His right arm and shoulder were feeling worse and looking at the cliffs he was doubtful whether he would be able to save himself anyway. However, he managed to climb off the rock where the car was, and clamber towards the cliff. He slumped down in the shelter of the cliff face and watched as a sudden gust of wind and large wave carried the car off the rock and into the raging sea. The noise of the wind and rain obscured that of metal on rock as it slid to a watery grave.

He was cold and still bleeding from the head. His arm and shoulder hurt and his bruised legs were painful. However, he realised that staying put was not an option. He hauled himself up and started to climb over the rocks towards a point where the cliff seemed lowest. Reaching that point he saw a ledge above him from which he thought he would be able to get back to the road. With a huge feat of will he managed to get up onto the ledge, but the effort was too much for him to continue. He squashed himself into the cliff face on the ledge and closed his eyes. As he fell into unconsciousness he was not sure he ever wanted to wake up.

Early the following morning the sun was shining as Stan opened his eyes. He remembered where he was, and the events of the previous day. The bleeding from his head had stopped but his arm and shoulder still hurt and his legs ached. His clothes had dried overnight as the storm had abated and the early morning sun shone. He was a little surprised to find that he was still on this ledge; clearly no one had come looking for him. That suited him, as he had no intention of returning to The Haven. The crushed car with its broken windows and twisted metal was now visible above the retreating waves. He looked across the water, as still as a millpond, and it was difficult to imagine the raging of yesterday. He stood up and was pleased to find he was nearer to the level of the road than he had thought. He was able to climb up onto the road, and started to walk, albeit slowly, away from Seatown. He wanted to get away from the town without anyone knowing what had occurred. Being a bus driver meant that he could not catch a bus, as he would have been recognised, and he could not afford a taxi even if he could find one. He decided to hitch-hike. There was little likelihood of getting a lift on the road from the house, but if he could make his way to the Exeter road, that should be easier. There was no traffic at all until he came to the junction with the road to Exeter, then he stood at the crossroads, hoping for a friendly driver. A big Foden lorry slowed as the driver saw Stan.

'Where to, mate?'

'Exeter, if you're going that far,' replied Stan. 'Thanks.'

'Come on then, get in.'

Stan lifted himself up into the driver's cab, explaining that he had had a fall and hurt his shoulder and arm. The lorry driver was not interested, but chatted on about the Test matches against Pakistan.

Stan was happy. He was a cricket fan and much preferred to talk about that, than how he came to be in such a state.

Things were looking up for Stan Proctor.

Chapter Twenty Eight

Madeleine was unsure how to tell Tina and Kevin the full story of Stan and Eric. She and Ian had invited them for a cup of tea the following Sunday afternoon. A chilly wind had blown up which prevented Madeleine serving it in the garden, which she had thought would have been more to Tina's liking. She decided it was now time to take the plunge;

'Tina,' she said, 'what do you know about the incident known as the Haven Horror Road accident?'

'Same as everybody else, I suppose. Bloke was driving along the road and a landslide pushed him and his car over the edge and he was killed. What else is there to know?'

'I didn't know there was any more to it than that,' agreed Kevin.

'Well,' said Madeleine, 'I have been doing some digging. It seems that the man who was pushed over the cliff didn't die.'

'How do you know that?' asked Tina.

Madeleine told her how the newspaper reports had referred to the accident but had not reported any details about a body being found.

'They don't always know, though, do they? They make half of it up, anyway.'

Tina's opinion of the press was as low as her opinion of the church.

'Anyway, what's it got to do with me and my Dad?'

'I'll explain why. I think that your dad was the man who went over the cliff. He survived the fall and left Seatown. Then, some years later, he came back and married your mum.'

Tina looked at Madeleine open-mouthed. Then tears burst forth and she sobbed into Kevin's shoulder. He tried calming her down but it was impossible. She clung tightly to Kevin as her chest heaved with the effort of crying. Madeleine and Ian sat silently, letting the information sink in slowly. Tina pulled out tissue after tissue as she sought to stop the flow. Eventually the sobbing stopped, and wiping her eyes and nose she looked up at Madeleine, her face red from the tears.

'Tell me again,' she spluttered, 'tell me again what you just said.'

Madeleine explained again how Stan Proctor was the man who had gone over the cliff, and survived.

'But my Dad was Eric Smith, and I was Tina Smith. Does this mean I am really Tina Proctor?'

'Let me tell you the full story,' said Madeleine.

She took out the birth certificates of Stan and Doreen, and the marriage certificates of Stan and Edna, and Eric and Sylvia.

'You remember I phoned you and asked you if your dad had been born in Dorset?'

'Yes.'

'That was because I couldn't find his birth. The reason I couldn't find his birth was that he was born Stan Proctor. Then I bought the marriage certificates of Stan and Eric, and you can see how similar the details are. Obviously the surname is different, and he has chosen a new Christian name, but everything else is very similar. You told me how your dad liked to read Old Testament stories; look at the change between Stan's father's name and Eric's father's. David and Jonathan, see?'

Madeleine gave Tina more details about the discoveries she had made, including her speculation about Stan's life after the accident. She did say that it was only speculation but Tina was keen to grab hold of any redeeming feature in the story.

'So Dad came back to Seatown to look after his dying sister?'

'We're not sure of that, but it seems likely. Otherwise there would seem to have been no reason to return. She died a couple of years after he came back, then he met your mum and married her.'

'But he was married already, wasn't he? As Stan?'

'It looks like it, yes. There may have been a divorce, I don't know. When he married your mum he said he was a bachelor.'

'That makes him a bigamist, then,' cried Tina.

Tina burst into tears again.

Kevin held her close and comforted her. Madeleine continued;

'When Stan came back to Seatown it is most likely that he changed his name by Deed Poll; that would make life easier with bureaucracy, banks, the taxman and so on. If he did execute a Deed Poll, then it must be somewhere. He would have used it initially to inform various organisations, and then he would have kept it.'

'There was nothing in the box the home gave us,' said Kevin, 'only those bits we gave to you.'

'There is one possibility,' said Ian, 'solicitors very often keep documents which they have prepared for clients. Once Eric had sent the document to the bank and the taxman he might have left it with the solicitor who drew it up.'

'That's tricky,' said Kevin, 'it's over fifty years ago. How many solicitors have closed down in that time?'

'If the one Eric used has closed, then everything that they had would have been transferred to another firm, especially if they were unable to make contact with the client concerned,' said Ian. 'Anyway let's be positive, which solicitors who were around fifty years ago are still in the town today?'

'Don't look at me,' said Madeleine, 'I'm new.'

'I don't have a clue,' said Tina.

'Nor me,' agreed Kevin.

'Tomorrow I shall phone one of the firms and ask them; they'll know. Some old buffer who's been there since Dickens will be able to give me chapter and verse,' said Ian. 'Now, more tea and cake anyone?'

The mood had lightened, and Ian and Madeleine could now talk more easily about the ins and outs of Stan's case. Then Tina suddenly burst out;

'That's it, I just realised, he was married, wasn't he?'

'Who?' asked Kevin.

'This Stan.'

'Yes, why?' answered Madeleine

'The receipt, it's for his wedding ring to, what was her name?'

'Edna,' said Madeleine

Madeleine and Ian looked at each other in disbelief. How could they have overlooked such an obvious answer to the query about the shop receipt?

The next day Ian rang round the local solicitors. None of them was very helpful, either not knowing who was in business all those years ago, which was not surprising, or couldn't be bothered even to listen, which was annoying. Ian looked down his list; Shaw, Shaw, Shaw and Johnson, Market Place, Seatown, I'll try them, he thought. I might get to speak to Mr Shaw.

'Good morning, SSSJ can I help you?'

Ian was irritated by the constant use of initials in company names, it didn't tell you who they were, he thought.

'Can I speak to Mr Shaw, please?'

'Which Mr Shaw would you like to speak to, Mr Charles or Mr Henry?'

'Mr Charles, please,' said Ian. He had no reason to ask this, but guessed that the more senior of the two would have been mentioned first.

'One moment please,'

'Charles Shaw speaking.'

A gruff voice on the other end of the phone did not augur well, thought Ian.

'Good morning Mr Shaw, I wonder if you could help me. I am trying to find out which of the solicitors currently in the town were in business in the late 1950s. A friend of mine is trying to trace an item which would have been left with her father's solicitors sometime in the mid to late 1950s.'

The voice softened slightly.

'And you are?'

'Sorry, my name is Ian Clay.'

'Are you the Ian Clay who is in the choir at St Martin's?'

'Yes, I am.'

'Splendid, splendid. Always make such a good noise.'

The voice was now almost friendly.

'Yes, Mr Clay, we were here then. My great-grandfather Isaac Shaw started the firm in the 1880s. There has been a Shaw in the law, since 1884,' he chuckled at his own, rather old, joke.

'Which other firms were there? Of course the papers might have been left with a firm that's closed since,' said Ian.

'Yes, that's true. But you might as well start with the ones that are still around. The only other firm in the town then and now is Hughes and Lewis; old Jeremiah Lewis and my twin brother Henry and I all started to practise at about the same time in the mid-fifties. What were you looking for?'

'A packet or parcel with a document in, in the name of Eric Smith, probably left with you in 1959/60.'

'Not us, then,' said Charles. 'We had very small offices in those years. In 1961 we had our present office built, so we had more storage space. We had been unable to retain documents for clients since 1958. We barely had room for our own files.'

'Thank you Mr Shaw, you have been very helpful. And thank you for your kind remarks about the choir, I shall pass that on to my fellow choristers.'

Ian replaced the handset. He remembered the name of Hughes and Lewis from his conversation with John Williams. It was they who were the solicitors involved with this will he was so anxious about. What a coincidence. Then he thought, no it isn't, they are a very old-established firm in the town. Lots of local people will have dealings with them. But he couldn't dispel the notion that it was more than a coincidence.

He picked up the phone again and dialled the number of Hughes and Lewis. He got the usual greeting and request. He asked to speak to Mr Jeremiah Lewis, but was told, politely but firmly, that he did not deal with new clients these days. He was put through to the general office and spoke to a bright young man, clearly eager to help.

'Yes, we have been here many years, and yes we do keep documents and packages for clients,' he said. 'What name are you looking for?'

Ian told him and the bright young man, whose name Ian discovered was George, confirmed the existence of a small package in that name.

'However, I have to tell you, 'he said, 'you will not be able to gain access to it. Only the depositor of the parcel or the executor of their will could have access.'

Ian explained that the depositor was dead and enquired whether the next of kin could have the package.

'We would need to see the death certificate and also a grant of probate to that person, together, of course, with that person identifying him or herself satisfactorily.'

'I will speak to my friend,' said Ian, disappointed at this hurdle to be overcome, 'I am not sure what the situation is with regard to a will and probate. I will be in touch again.'

'Thank you, we'll look forward to hearing from you,' said George, and with that the call was over. Ian was feeling cross that he could make no more progress. He had been hoping to settle the matter of the deed poll swiftly, but now it was clear that was not to be the case.

He reported back to Madeleine and then spoke to Tina, who told him that her dad had made a will and left everything to her, although, as she pointed out, there was precious little to leave. Tina had done nothing about proving the will and Ian suggested that she and Kevin, and he if she so chose, should make an appointment with bright young George at Hughes and Lewis to ask them to deal with the will. She agreed immediately, and Ian made the necessary arrangements. It was not going to be quick; but then, pondered Ian, has anyone ever met a lawyer who does anything quickly?

Chapter Twenty Nine

He had put it off for days, and still couldn't decide what to do. John Williams was going to speak to Madeleine Porter about the child whom he thought should have been the beneficiary under Mary's will. But he knew that if he made the phone call, he would have to reveal more than he had ever wished to.

He walked into his bedroom, opened the wardrobe and pushed aside the racks of suits, revealing a small safe. He keyed in the combination and opened the door, taking out a small bundle of papers. Undoing the tie around them he looked at the writing on the outside of the envelope, that familiar writing which he had always enjoyed seeing, but this letter was different. This letter was the one which had caused so much trouble and distress, and in one sense had led to the current problem.

He recalled how, when this letter had arrived, he had been out at the corn market with his father. His mother had misread the name of John on the envelope as Joan, her name. When she opened the letter and read it, she realised that it was for him, not her, but the damage had been done. John and his father arrived back from the market after lunch, having had a drink in the pub with the other farmers. They were in a good mood, having had a successful sale of their produce, and an enjoyable chat with their farmer friends.

As soon as he walked in the door John could see that something was wrong. His mother was a short spare woman, with light brown hair cut close to her head. John was her only child and she had doted on him. She had been brought up as a strict Methodist, and she saw the world in very black and white terms. She knew that her son was a good-looking young man, and that he had a way with the girls, but she had not expected this.

John's father spoke first;

'What's up? You look as if you've seen a ghost.'

Still unable to form any words in her rage, she threw the letter across the room. John recognised the writing as it fell on to the floor.

'Ask him,' she shouted, pointing at John. 'I'm ashamed of you. Get out.'

John tried to speak but was shouted down by his mother, who had now found her full voice.

'Get out! Get out, and never come back! Neither your father nor I ever want to see you again. Get out! Get your clothes and leave immediately. Now!'

John cowered before this onslaught, realising that resistance was futile. He slunk upstairs, turning as he did so;

'Mother.'

'Get out!'

He went upstairs and gathered his few belongings together, put them in an old case he had in his room and came back downstairs.

'Get out,' she shouted again.

John's father, Thomas, had tried to speak to his wife while John had been upstairs, but she had just picked the letter up off the floor, handed it to him, and said nothing. As John walked out, Thomas said sadly;

'Goodbye, son. You'd better take this,' as he gave him the letter.

John Williams never saw his parents again after that day. Years later he heard that they had both died, his mother first, followed very quickly by his father. He returned to the farm to settle the estate and pick up their personal effects, and one or two things of his own, as well.

He looked again at the letter in his hand. How could one sheet of paper with a bit of ink on it cause such a rift? After his departure he had tried to contact his parents, but they were implacable. The writing on the envelope had been smudged, maybe it was a rainy day when it was posted or delivered. The stick of the 'h' was obscured and it did look like 'Joan' at first glance. He couldn't blame his mother for making that mistake, but even then he thought her reaction was unreasonable. He took the paper out of the envelope and started to read;

2 September 1954

My dearest John,

I am writing to you now that I have come home from hospital. It has been very difficult this last week or so. I was told about the accident on the road involving Stan, but I haven't heard any more. The paper tried to speak to me but I told them I didn't want to say anything. Do you know what happened to Stan? Has he been back to the house? There was nothing in the paper about a body being found, was there?

I have got one bit of news which I found out whilst I was in hospital. I am expecting a baby, in April next year. I know it isn't yours, we have always been so careful. I wonder what Stan would have thought about becoming a father. I don't regret what we did for one moment. You cared for me in a way he never did. You kissed me in a way he never did. You loved me in a way he never did. I shall always have happy memories of our time together. I don't know what will happen now, I suppose Stan might come back, but if not I shall have to try to carry on as best I can. Write to me when you can, but probably better not to come here at the moment.

All my love

Edna xxx

John folded the letter carefully and put it back in its envelope. Tears welled up inside him as he remembered her. After he had left home he did not write to her as he did not wish to make a bad situation worse. His mother was clearly upset with the discovery that he was having an affair with a married woman, and while he felt he could justify his actions, there seemed no way back, either with his mother or Edna.

Now she was pregnant he thought that any more involvement on his part might indicate that he was the father, which he was equally as sure as she was, that he was not. When he left home he found various casual jobs before settling outside Chippenham, working as a rep for a company selling paper bags to shops. This was the start of his long road to striking out on his own, with a small loan from the bank, as a packaging supplier, and ultimately to PPS. As he stood in the bedroom with the envelope in his hand he thought how he would have given up everything for Edna. If she had not been pregnant at that time with Stan's baby, he felt sure they would have been together, but it was pointless speculating, it wasn't to be.

He put the envelope away, closed the safe, and went downstairs to make that phone call.

'Madeleine Porter speaking,'

'Hello, Mrs Porter, can I call you Madeleine? Thanks. You know that I asked Ian Clay and you to do a bit of work for me, which was unsuccessful; well I am ringing to apologise. I did not give you full information, which was unfair of me. I did it for selfish reasons which I can now see were foolish. I think it would be a good idea if we had another chat and I told you what is going on, so that you will, hopefully, be able to resolve the conundrum I posed. Would you mind if I came to The Haven?'

Madeleine was taken aback, as she had not really expected any further contact from John Williams on the matter. In fact she was not sure she wanted to have any further involvement. Her previous experience with people on matters such as these had showed her that there is a necessity to be completely open and above-board. If that trust was not there, then the whole exercise was pointless. Her irritation came through when she spoke to him.

'John,' she said, 'I am going to speak plainly. I was disappointed that you didn't feel able to trust me first time around with confidential information. I have no problem with you wanting to keep your business to yourself, but if you want me to investigate this type of thing then you have to be open with me. I can't do it with one hand tied behind my back. I am only willing to carry on with your full assurance of openness and honesty. I will not pry, but if I need to know something to solve the problem I expect you to tell me. I know this sounds harsh, but it is the only way to do this type of business.'

John Williams knew she was right, and she was also right to put it so plainly. He was chastened by her remarks, and he knew he would not do the same again.

'You are completely right,' he said. 'Will you take me on again if I give you that undertaking? Please?'

'Yes, I will. It would be a good idea for you to come to The Haven. I hope you don't mind if Ian joins us,' she added, only out of politeness; she would not have said she would do it if he had said no.'

'Of course not,' he agreed,' when would be best?'

'I will check with Ian, but next Sunday afternoon, probably. Come then if I don't contact you beforehand.'

'Next Sunday then, thank you. Goodbye.'

Madeleine was pleased to hear from him, as it would help her to continue her investigation into the cuckoo clock story. She was not sure whether to raise it with him on Sunday; perhaps she would ask Ian's opinion. She found she was asking his opinion on many things nowadays. She wondered what more John Williams had to say about the child, and what had led up to the enquiry he was making.

Chapter Thirty

Joseph was getting used to his new home, and his new parents were getting used to him. Fiona and Tim were revelling in their new parenthood, enjoying the admiring glances of friends and neighbours. Fiona found that she could sit for ages just looking at him when he was asleep, marvelling in the perfection of every part of him. Madeleine had been keeping her up-to-date with her investigations, and as Fiona watched Joseph she thought of Edna. She could not comprehend how Edna must have felt when her baby died; the loss and devastation would be total, she thought. It would be enough to test anyone's faith, if they had any, and for those of no faith, it would reinforce their view of the world as a hostile place.

In her last email Madeleine had said how John Williams was going to come back for a further discussion, and she asked Fiona what she thought would be the best course of action. Fiona had been keeping a close eye on developments in Seatown, so she was well able to offer advice. She fully endorsed Madeleine's firm line with him, and said that she should not allow him any further leeway, and that she fully understood her position. She said that, when Williams came on Sunday, Madeleine must make it crystal clear that this was his last chance to tell her everything he knew. In addition to this advice in her email, Fiona sent a series of pictures of Joseph looking angelic asleep in his crib, and gorgeous when awake. Madeleine was moved to tears of happiness.

Before the Sunday meeting with John Williams, Ian had called to see Madeleine, and they had discussed how to approach him. Madeleine showed Ian Fiona's email and he concurred with her advice. As they were chatting they heard the soft purr of an expensive engine, as Williams' Jaguar pulled up outside.

As he came into the house the greetings from Madeleine and Ian were rather more formal, but still polite. They sat down in the living room, tea and coffee was provided, and Madeleine started to speak. Before she could utter a word John spoke;

'I'm sorry. I'll say it again, I'm sorry. I know I messed you around last time and I don't want to do the same again. When we first met I thought we were going to get on well, and I would like to think that we can get back to that.'

'Thank you, John. I agree. Let's start from now. So what would you like me, or us should I say, to do?'

'As I told you before, I had a conversation with my solicitor, Jeremiah Lewis, who told me I was the beneficiary under the will of a Mary Treacy, who was an old friend. I was surprised by this because I thought that Mary had had a child, and I would have thought that he or she would have inherited.'

'Maybe they had fallen out, or lost contact. Maybe the child is dead. How long ago did you say it was? Mid-fifties wasn't it?' said Madeleine.

'Yes, that's right. 1955. When we spoke last time I said that I wasn't sure of the sex of the child, but that is not true, it was a boy. I only learned it was a boy many years later. I think he was born in Seatown.'

'Do you know anything else?' asked Ian, 'it's not much to go on.'

'No, it isn't. What I do know is that his mother, Mary, went abroad for a time, I presume she took the boy with her.'

'Could he be abroad? Even if his mother came back to England he may have stayed wherever it was. If she moved a long time ago he would have grown up there.'

'That's very possible,' agreed John. 'She worked for many years as a translator in France. But even so why would she not leave him her estate?'

'Maybe he's dead?' suggested Ian

'Possible. I wouldn't know. The will was dated only last year. Maybe there was a previous will naming him, he died, and then she made a new one.'

'Let's assume he's dead,' said Madeleine, 'why would she name you?'

'This is guesswork,' said John, 'but I don't think she has any other living family. I am pretty certain she was an only child, and her parents will be long dead, of course.'

'Who was the father of the child? Was she ever married? Why isn't he the beneficiary?' asked Madeleine, determined to find out as much as possible. Even with his promise of openness she was not sure he was telling the full story.

'I think she was married many years ago, and so I expect he was the boy's father. It's a long time ago, but I think her husband was a lot older than her, so he's probably been dead for years.'

'When we had a chat before, I checked out the births marriages and deaths records for Treacy, and I could find nothing which seemed to match. No Treacy birth in 1955 and no Treacy marriage locally. They may have married elsewhere, but it's difficult to check without more details. Without more information I am not sure that there is much more I can do,' said Madeleine. 'There may be some mileage in the overseas connection. Do you know when she went to France?'

'I am not sure. I think it was mid to late fifties. If I am right the boy would have been very young. Sorry I can't be any more help. The money is rightly mine under the will, but I just feel bad about taking it if there is someone else who ought to have it. But if you can't find him then that's it.'

John Williams stood up to leave and Madeleine was undecided whether to tell him of their discoveries about the clock. She was sure there was more that he was not telling, so she opted for not saying anything now. There would be further opportunities, she was sure.

'Thank you Madeleine, and Ian. I will not harass you for a result. Just tell me when you have something to report.'

He shook hands and left

'Why did he bother?' asked Ian with exasperation. 'He told us no more than last time. Apart from the fact that the mother went abroad. What I don't understand is why he is so bothered about it. Someone leaves him a flat and savings worth what, over a hundred thousand, and he's fretting over some boy who in his view should have it. If his mother wanted him to have it, she would have left it to him.'

'Forget about him just for a moment. Let's consider other possibilities. He said that the boy's mother went abroad, and then he said she worked as a translator in France for many years. If so, let's see if we can find her travelling to France,' said Madeleine.

'How can you do that?' asked Ian.

'Back to the family history websites. They have passenger lists of people leaving the UK up to 1960.'

'That's handy,' said Ian.

'We might be lucky,' said Madeleine, 'but cross channel trips are not included, so we might not find her. But if she went on a ship bound for, say, Australia, and that ship called at a French port, then she would be listed.'

'Go on then. Fingers crossed.'

Madeleine searched for Mary Treacy travelling to France in the late 1950s but could find nothing.

'Even if she did, then, she must have gone on a cross channel ferry. Shame. It had been a good idea.'

'Try Edna,' suggested Ian.

'Why Edna? Do you think she and Mary are one and the same? I suppose it might explain why John Williams has been so reluctant to tell us much. Here goes.'

She keyed in Edna Proctor, travelling to France between 1955 and 1960.

'Look at that! Edna Proctor on a ship to South Africa, the Stirling Castle, disembarking at Marseille on 21 November 1955. Travelling alone. That was very brave. Where did she get the money from? Maybe old Stan didn't trust banks and put it under the mattress,' said Madeleine.

'Well, wherever she got the money from, I am sure that is the right person. It even gives her age. And there is no one travelling with her. Surely she couldn't speak French, could she?'

'Very unlikely,' said Ian, 'maybe she was a bright girl who wanted to learn. It's surprising how quickly you can pick up a language when you have to. If you live among people speaking it all the time, it wouldn't take long.'

'What about papers? Wouldn't she need something to allow her to live there?' asked Madeleine.

'Initially she would have her passport. After that she could apply to stay for longer if she had a job which was essential, perhaps. If she learnt quickly she might get a job as a translator quite easily in a port like Marseille.'

'Well, now we know what happened to Edna and Stan. Why is John Williams being so mysterious? Working on the basis that Stan does not return, Edna goes to France and Paul is dead, we have accounted for all the family. What we haven't accounted for is the cuckoo clock, and John Williams' involvement in this whole business.'

'And 1510,' reminded Ian.

'Yes, I'd forgotten that. Of course that is now relevant to Stan now as well as Eric.'

The clock cuckooed the hour, six o'clock. Madeleine went into the kitchen.

'Are you staying for a bite?' she called through to Ian.

'If you'll have me,' he said with a smile.

'A pleasure,' she replied, as she put the kettle on and started to prepare some food.

Some sandwiches made, the tea poured and the cake ready to cut, Ian and Madeleine sat in the living room, enjoying the evening sunshine. The cuckoo clock looked down on them, challenging them to solve the puzzle which had baffled Madeleine since before she had even moved in. From the moment that she had exclaimed her liking of the clock on that first day when she had met John Williams, she had been engrossed in trying to find out its history. She had now discovered that the clock had been posted to John Williams, shortly before Paul's death. She had yet to find out whether it had been posted from The Haven, but she strongly suspected that it had. In that case Edna Proctor had sent the clock to John Williams. Why? That was what she still wanted to uncover. John Williams, she thought, was the only person to be able to answer that question, and he was a reluctant contributor to this quest.

'So is that what John Williams was trying not to tell us?' asked Madeleine.

'What? That Mary is Edna? Probably,' said Ian. 'That means also, that if Edna is Mary, then Mary is Paul's mother. Is Paul therefore the child that John Williams is searching for, or is there another one? If there isn't, then the reason John Williams is named as the beneficiary in this will is that Paul is dead, and he does not know that.'

'When did Edna go to France?' asked Madeleine.

'November 1955, just after Paul dies. If he doesn't know that Paul is dead, then he can't have had any contact with her since 1955. There is no child listed on the passenger list in November, but a babe in arms might not be listed separately.'

'That's right' said Madeleine, 'but is there another possibility. Did Edna have a child, perhaps fathered by John, before she married Stan? Did Stan discover this? Was that why he left?'

'If that's the case, then where is the child? She can't have had two children who died, surely? That would be too unkind.'

'Adopted?' suggested Madeleine. 'Let's look them up.'

Scrutinising the births website she could find no record of any children born in Seatown by the name of Proctor or Fox at the appropriate time.

'No, doesn't look like it. I think that we have solved Mr Williams' query without his help; but I still think there is more to it.

Chapter Thirty One

'Are you coming this morning?' called Tina, from the bedroom.

'I can't hear, I'm in the shower.'

Tina got out of bed and padded along the landing to the bathroom where Kevin was getting ready for work. Pushing the door open she said again;

'Are you coming today? You know; the solicitors. Madeleine made that appointment to go and see them about Dad's will, and this deed poll thing.'

Kevin turned the shower off and stepped out, drying his hair.

'I've got to go to Dorchester at eleven for a meeting at the council offices. All to do with reorganising our work loads. In other words, who can we make redundant most easily? Well it won't be me. When's the appointment with the solicitors?'

'Half past ten.'

'Sorry, I've got to go this morning. Otherwise it will be me if I don't even turn up. Madeleine'll look after you. She knows what she's doing.'

'OK, then, but I'd prefer it if you were coming. Shall I try and change the date?'

'Trouble is, said Kevin, 'if you do that, you never know when you will be able to rearrange for. And even then I might not be able to get there. You go, and if there's anything you're not sure of, don't sign it, tell me and then I'll ring them tomorrow if necessary.'

'Thanks,' she said and kissed him.

Kevin walked back to the bedroom to get dressed as Tina got into the shower. As she looked at her skinny frame and considered her poor skin, she could not understand what it was about her that attracted Kevin. She was so lucky, she thought, having such a wonderful man.

She waved Kevin off to work and wished him good luck. She knew that, whatever he said about it not being him, it was always a worrying time when reorganisation was in the air. And whilst she didn't want it to be Kevin, she knew there would be someone going home tonight, or on the phone later, with bad news, and her heart went out to them.

The door bell rang at exactly ten o'clock; Madeleine was always very punctual. Tina was ready for her and picked up her bag, making sure she had with her the pieces of paper she needed. Ian was busy that morning as well, so it was just the two women who arrived at the offices of Hughes and Lewis. They sat in the reception area, waiting for George Hastings, the young man whom Madeleine had spoken to on the phone. The office was clean and smart. The walls were freshly painted, the carpet and the furniture new, and the brisk efficiency of the staff matched the overall appearance of a modern firm not hidebound by old-fashioned practices.

A door opened and a young man in his early thirties stepped through. He was shaven-headed with a stud earring in his right ear, sharp suit and dark blue shirt set off by a pale pink tie.

'Good morning, I'm George Hastings,' he said, coming across to where Madeleine and Tina were seated.

'Hello. Mr Hastings,' said Tina hesitantly,' I'm Tina Jenkins, and this is my friend Madeleine Porter.'

'Hello, Mrs Jenkins, hello Mrs Porter. Do call me George, by the way. Do come this way.'

He guided them through the door and into a small office off the corridor. It was comfortably furnished with a desk, a swivel chair, and two chairs for the clients. A bright plant grew in the corner, which Madeleine noticed was, unusually for office plants, well cared for.

'Take a seat; now what can I do for you.'

Tina asked Madeleine to do the talking, and she explained again about the small packet which was being held by the solicitor. Tina handed George the death certificate of her father, together with the will which he had made. George took a few moments to read through the will. It had been made in 2001, after the divorce from Sylvia, and left all his possessions to Tina.

'Did your father own his own house,' asked George.

'No, we always lived in rented or council places. I think he had a bit of money in the bank, but not much. He was in the Laurels for the last three years, so that took his pension.'

'Yes, I see. Leave it with me Mrs Jenkins, and I will sort it out for you. It looks quite straightforward. Now you were asking about a packet which you said we have.'

'That's right. I believe my father was born Stanley Proctor, but then changed his name to Eric Smith. We, Mrs Porter and I, are guessing that in that packet will be a deed poll document which shows that change of name. Do you have it there?'

'We do,' said George, 'there is something slightly odd about it. Unlike banks we don't allocate numbers to the parcels we keep for clients. We just file them under the client's name. Always have done, and we find it much easier that way. Now this parcel has writing on the outside which I don't understand. I'll show you.'

George produced a long brown envelope, the shape of a legal document, which was sealed at both ends. On the outside was written;

1510 Jeremiah 21:14

'Have you any idea what this relates to?' asked George. 'Our senior partner is Jeremiah Lewis, but it's nothing to do with him, I asked him.'

'When the nursing home gave me dad's personal belongings, there was a small envelope which contained a sheet of paper with the number 1510 written on it. We have been trying to work out what it means but have not yet come up with the answer. This doesn't seem to help.'

'Do you have a Bible?' asked Madeleine.

George looked dumbfounded.

'Er, I don't know. I think so.'

He left the room and disappeared along the corridor. A few moments later he came back with a New Testament.

'Will this do? It was all I could find.'

'No,' said Madeleine. 'Jeremiah is a book of the Old Testament. I think this is a biblical quote. Can we take the envelope?'

'Not at present,' said George, 'as soon as I have completed the estate then you will be able to. I'll write down those numbers for you, if you would like me to.'

'Thank you,' said Madeleine.

George jotted the numbers on a piece of paper and gave it to Tina.

'I'll be in touch as soon as I can. Thank you very much.'

Tina and Madeleine left the office intrigued by this additional clue in the puzzle.

'Let's go along to the church and see if I am right about the quotation,' said Madeleine, and she hurried through the rain which was starting to fall. They got into the porch just as it was coming on harder, and opening the door they were greeted by Ian, doing his stewarding. It had been a quiet morning, and Ian was glad of the company.

'Come and sit down over here,' he said, indicating three chairs placed around a small table in the back corner of the church. 'I can keep an eye on the door from here, while you tell me about your visit to the solicitors.'

Madeleine explained the process which Tina would have to go through to prove the will, and therefore be allowed to take away the package held by Hughes and Lewis. She also told him about the writing on the envelope, and said they had called in to check the quotation, to see if it would give them a clue to the mysterious number, 1510.

'What was the reference,' said Ian, picking up a bible from one of the pews.

'Jeremiah, chapter twenty one, verse fourteen,' said Madeleine.

Ian found the passage. 'This will be the one, ''I will punish you as your deeds deserve, declares the Lord.'' Sounds a bit severe. What was that number again? 1510? Is that the time, ten minutes past three in the afternoon? Is he saying that he is punishing Edna or is he being punished, and if so for what?'

'Just a minute,' said Madeleine, 'is that a new translation? Would the old one be the same?'

She found the quotation in an Authorised Version where it was slightly different, but with the same meaning.

''I don't think there is any doubt what he is saying here. Edna deserves punishing, and he is carrying that out.'

Tina was sitting in silence during this exchange, wondering how her father could have behaved in such a way.

'I know he had a temper, she said, 'like I told you. But this sounds a lot worse than a few cross words.'

'Edna was pregnant, wasn't she, at the time of the accident? Is Stan saying here that he is punishing Edna because he is not the father?' asked Ian.

'We don't know whether Stan knew she was expecting, or even if Edna herself knew come to that,' said Madeleine. 'But what else might he feel that he had to punish her for? Punish is a very strong word.'

'Don't forget,' said Ian, 'it was the early 1950s. Times were different. If a husband hit his wife occasionally, then no one thought any more about it. The police would certainly not be interested.'

'No, but this is more than 'giving her a slap',' said Madeleine. 'He has kept a piece of paper with the time written on it, and he has also written it on the outside of a sealed envelope deposited with a firm of solicitors. This, in Stan's eyes, is surely more serious than his normal behaviour.'

'Dad never hit Mum,' said Tina, 'at least, I never saw him. Like I said he'd get very cross sometimes, but I am sure he didn't hit her.'

'Times change, and people change with them sometimes,' said Ian, 'maybe after this incident, whatever it entailed, he changed how he treated women.'

'It doesn't get us very far though, does it,' asked Madeleine. 'We now know what the number represents, or at least we think we do, but we don't know what happened on that fateful day, either in the run-up to the accident, or immediately afterwards.'

'We know that Stan ran away, survived the accident, and that he returned about six or seven years later to look after his sister, then marry Sylvia and have Tina. I am not sure what else there is to know,' said Ian.

'What else there is to know is what was going on at ten minutes past three on the day of the accident that made him want to record it forever? It must have been something major, whatever it was. But who else is likely to know the answer to that? Stan is dead, Edna is dead. Who's left?' said Madeleine.

'No one,' said Ian. 'The only possibility is John Williams. I'm not saying he was there, but he is the only person we know of who had even a slight connection with the incident. We know that Edna, or Mary, left her estate to him. That must mean something. Maybe he can fill in the details.'

'The last two occasions we have spoken to him he has been uncooperative, and that was when he wanted us to do something for him. Why should he want to help us solve our little mystery?' said Madeleine.

'If he knew my dad's first wife,' said Tina, 'surely we can ask him what he knows about what happened to her. Anyway, if they never divorced he was still Edna's husband until he died. That must mean something. It seems to me that Dad was involved with something on that day, and it may not be very nice, I don't know, but I want to know what it was.'

Tina's face was set firm and both Madeleine and Ian were surprised to see this side of her. She had always seemed to be such a mouse. Maybe there was something of Stan in her after all.

'I agree with you, Tina,' said Madeleine, 'this has gone on for long enough. We, and I mean all three of us, will speak to Mr Williams. This time I am not going to allow him to fob us off. We, especially Tina, need to know the whole truth.'

With that a small group of visitors came into the church and Ian stood up and went across to greet them. While he was dealing with them, Madeleine and Tina went to leave.

'I'll let you know that date,' Madeleine called to Ian, and he waved in acknowledgement.

She dropped Tina off at home and drove back to The Haven. On her arrival she checked the phone messages and found one from Fiona.

'Just letting you know everything is OK. I was ringing to arrange a visit. Give me a call and let me know. I hope you have still got that cuckoo clock for young Joseph to enjoy.'

Madeleine cast her mind back to the conversation she had had with Fiona and Tim before Joseph was born, when Fiona had said she was sure that the little one would like the clock. Now we will see, she thought. She was delighted that they all wanted to visit, and phoned back straight away. They fixed a date for a fortnight hence, and Madeleine told her that she was hopeful of an end to her cuckoo clock quest by then, and she could tell her the full story. As she was saying this Madeleine was keeping her fingers crossed at the same time. That, she thought, is going to depend on John Williams.

He was the next call she made. When they had last spoken it had been agreed that Madeleine would contact him when there was news to relay. He was still anxious about the Mary Treacy will, and Madeleine was now confident she had the answer to that, and the details of the child whom he thought should inherit. However, she did not want to have that conversation on the telephone. She also told him that, in addition to Ian, there would be a third person at the meeting, a Tina Jenkins. Arrangements were made and Madeleine rang off.

John Williams was curious. Madeleine Porter had said nothing on the phone, but the tone of her voice told him that there was something afoot. He was also curious about Tina Jenkins. Who was she? Was she the rightful heir, in his mind, to Mary Treacy's estate? He knew that Mary's child was a boy, so was this Tina his wife? Had he died and was she his widow? Thoughts whirled around in his head. He knew that he had not been completely open, but he determined that this time was going to be different.

With this in mind he went into his bedroom and opened the wardrobe. Upon opening the safe he took out the bundle of papers as he had done before, but this time he kept them all out. He hadn't read them all for such a long time, but he thought he must do so now. The shame that he felt swept over him as he sat on the bed, shame which he had lived with all these years. It was a shame that he could never share with Carole, or with anyone. Clearly Mary had forgiven him, or he would not have been named in the will, but that did not assuage the guilt he felt. Now he was going to have to face up to it, once and for all. He would face his demons and defeat them.

He put the papers safely into his briefcase ready for the meeting on Thursday. Eight o'clock at The Haven. He wondered how he was going to survive the next couple of days. He made himself an evening meal and sat and looked at it on the plate in front of him. He picked at the vegetables but couldn't eat it. He poured himself a drink, but it tasted bitter in his mouth. Nothing was right, and it was only Tuesday, he had forty eight hours to go.

On the following day he had a phone call from Jeremiah.

'I've received an offer on the flat, John. Thought I'd better check it out with you, but I think it's a good one. £95000. If it were up to me I'd take it,' he said.

'It is up to you, isn't it? You're the executor, so it's your decision.'

'I know, but as I said, I wanted to run it past you first. By the way there was £7700 in an ISA and about £3000 in a savings account with the bank. The shares which she held were worthless. The company had gone bankrupt years ago. The total value of the estate is going to be in the region of £100,000 after costs.'

'Yes, thank you, Jeremiah' said John, distractedly, 'yes, do that.'

'Are you OK, John, you don't sound at all well?'

'Sorry, Jeremiah, something's come up which is rather difficult for me. It'll be sorted tomorrow hopefully. I didn't mean to sound unfriendly. It's very good of you to keep me in the loop. That price sounds very good, I didn't think it would be that much, to be honest. Accept it.'

'Thank you John,' said Jeremiah, 'I hope everything works out satisfactorily tomorrow.'

'I am sure it will,' replied John, trying to be more optimistic, 'and if it does I expect I shall be coming to see you on another matter.'

'Look forward to it. Bye.'

Jeremiah Lewis hung up, and John Williams sat still, wishing he felt as confident as he had sounded on the phone.

Meanwhile Jeremiah Lewis was puzzled. Why had John Williams been so uninterested? Was it to do with that matter which he said he would not divulge, even to him? Time would tell.

Chapter Thirty One

Thursday arrived not a moment too soon for John Williams. He checked again that he had everything he needed for the meeting. The day dragged but eventually it was time for him to leave. He parked in the usual place at The Haven, and getting out of the car, Madeleine and Ian greeted him. On going in and sitting down he was introduced to a middle-aged woman named Tina Jenkins, whom he did not know, and her partner, Kevin. Madeleine explained that their part in the overall story would become clear.

Introductions over, and drinks provided, Madeleine spoke.

'Since moving in here a few months ago I have become interested in the history of the house, particularly the events surrounding the incident on the road into Seatown which has become known as the Haven Horror Road accident. When I started looking into this I found one or two anomalies which I couldn't understand; why did the newspaper report the absence of a body, at the time and later? Why was no mention made about the wife left behind on that fateful day, and what happened to her? Why were the police not more involved in the disappearance of Stan Proctor? And on a personal level what was the story of the cuckoo clock, which this house seems to have been furnished around? I first met John here as my new landlord, but then he asked me to research a beneficiary under a will. But he was reluctant to give me enough detail to be able to find an answer. Why? Then I met Tina and Kevin. Tina's father died recently and left a few belongings which contained an old shop receipt and an envelope with a mysterious set of numbers written on a piece of paper inside. At first Tina and Kevin did not appear to be connected with anything else, but that was not the case.'

'Madeleine,' interrupted John Williams, 'excuse me, can I say something, because if I tell you what I know, then you should be able to fit the other bits around it. As I go on, feel free to interrupt me and ask questions. There are parts of the story that I don't know, and hopefully your own investigations can fill those gaps.'

'Yes, John. A good idea,' said Madeleine.

John settled himself, opened his briefcase and took out various papers.

'I shall start right at the beginning. I was born in 1933. I was an only child and I grew up on a farm at Little Morton, just up the road. I went to the village school in Little Morton until I was eleven, and then I went on to the secondary school in Seatown. It was at the secondary school I first met Edna Fox. She was a very pretty girl, and, like most of the other boys, I was attracted to her. She was very slim, her hair was very dark brown, almost black and it was always cut in the latest fashion. Her face was like a pixy in a story book, with the most beautiful eyes you could ever hope to see. She lived with her mother and step-father in town. Her own father had died when she was only a toddler, but I believe she got on very well with her step-father.'

'Jean Sanders said that you were an admirer of hers,' said Ian.

'I wondered what she was saying when I saw you talking in the church that day. It all looked very clandestine,' said John.

'Not especially,' replied Ian, 'I think she was making more of it than there was.'

'I don't deny it. I think every boy would have gone out with her, given the chance. Anyway I was the lucky one. She was my first date; I was fourteen. I have loved her ever since. When she left school she got a job in a bakery shop on the market place in Seatown, and I went to help my father on the farm. Dad had spent his life working on the farm, first as a help to his dad, my grandfather, then on his own. He didn't own the farm, it was rented, but he still felt it was a family affair, and that I should take over from him in due course. It wasn't too bad at first, but then I wanted to break the ties a little bit. I started looking for other jobs, and that caused terrible rows at home. Dad thought I was deserting him and the family by wanting to leave the farm. He said we would lose the farm and the house. At the time, all I was interested in was getting a job away from home. I didn't say to him that another reason for wanting to leave the farm was that, if I found a job in Seatown, I would be able to see more of Edna.'

John paused and took a sip of his tea. His audience were listening intently, waiting to understand how this all fitted in with the other parts of the story. Tina looked up at the cuckoo clock, willing it to strike.

'The school leaving age had been raised to fifteen in 1947, so I left school in 1948. Constant battles, particularly with Dad, over working on the farm, eventually led to me getting a job on a building site two years later in 1950. That was my first, and maybe biggest, mistake.'

'National Service?' asked Ian.

'Spot on,' said John. 'When I was working on the farm I was exempt from being called up to do National Service. It was one of the so-called reserved occupations that the Government considered essential enough not to deprive it of its workers. Once I left the farm and started working on the building site in Seatown, I lost that exemption. It wasn't long before my call-up papers arrived in the post. Dad said that he had told me this would happen, but I didn't remember him saying so. Looking back, I think I was so keen to leave the farm that I wasn't really listening to any arguments put forward by him. So there I was, sent away to do military training, which I thought was a complete waste of time. Then Korea happened.'

'Sorry, what do you mean?' asked Tina.

'The Korean War, which started in June 1950 between North and South Korea. It was mainly fought by the USA and South Korea against China and North Korea, but that's a bit simplistic. From my point of view it was significant because Britain sent troops, including National Servicemen, to fight. One of those sent was me. If I had stayed on the farm I could have seen Edna occasionally; leaving the farm to try to be closer to her meant I could not see her at all, because I was called up and sent five and a half thousand miles away.'

'I didn't know that National Servicemen fought in Korea,' said Madeleine, 'were there many casualties?'

'Over one thousand British service personnel were killed, and many more wounded and missing.'

'That's dreadful, we never hear of them,' said Kevin.

'I know,' said John, 'I always think of them on Remembrance Day. I lost some good friends.'

'How sad,' said Tina, 'it's so easy to forget that the names on these War Memorials were real people. Dad was always a great supporter of Remembrance Day. Only day he ever went to church.'

'It's all very interesting, John, but where is this getting us?' asked Ian.

'I wanted to give you a bit of background to my relationship with Edna, so you can understand what happened and why. I was eighteen when I left for Korea. Edna was the same age. I loved her so much I can't tell you. I would go to sleep thinking of her, and she would be the first thing I thought about when I woke up the next day.'

He paused, and leant over to the pile of papers on the table. He took out a photograph of a young woman posing, leaning on a farm gate. He handed it round for them all to see. On the back of the photograph was written ILYEX. This was the first time Madeleine and Ian had ever seen a picture of Edna. John was right. She was the prettiest girl you could imagine.

'She's a lovely girl,' said Kevin. 'What are the letters on the back, can I ask?'

'Yes. The photo was taken shortly before I went away, and she gave it to me as a keepsake. The letters stand for I Love You Edna Kiss. We had been seeing each other regularly, and I suppose if we had been a bit older we would have got married before I left. We decided to leave it until my return.'

'Unfortunately my return was not as expected. Shortly after we arrived in Korea my unit was involved in a skirmish in which a number of my comrades were killed. I was wounded and taken prisoner. Regrettably, the Army got it wrong from thereon. They were convinced that I had been one of the fatalities. They had not been able at the time to recover the bodies of the fallen soldiers, and they sent a message back saying that I had been killed in action. I knew nothing of this until later, as I was unable to write letters because of my injuries. When the North Koreans reported their prisoners, as they had to, they said that they had a prisoner named William Johns.'

'As a result of this mix-up my parents received a notification from the Army that I had been killed. They were devastated, of course, as was Edna. I learnt later that it was twelve months before the error was corrected. By then Edna had married Stan, and it was all too late. I am sure you can understand how I felt when I discovered what had happened, and that Edna had married someone else. I always like to think it was because she was so upset at losing me that she married in haste, and sadly, came to repent at leisure.'

'How awful,' said Tina, 'couldn't you sue them or something?'

'It was awful, but there was nothing I could do. Edna was married to someone else, and suing the Army wouldn't have solved anything, and probably wasn't possible anyway. I was very bitter, but it wasn't Edna's fault. She had no way of knowing that the Army had got it wrong, and neither had Stan Proctor. It was just a bureaucratic bungle, but one with far-reaching effects.'

'So that's why Edna married Stan,' said Madeleine. 'The poor girl was ready for any shoulder to cry on, I should think.'

'When I returned from Korea and was discharged from the Army, I went back to work on the farm with Dad. He was pleased to have me back, obviously because he thought I was dead, but also because he liked having another man around the house. It was one day in Seatown market that I saw Edna for the first time after my return. Dad had told me that she had married and that she and her new husband were living at The Haven. One lunchtime I saw her coming out of the baker's shop where she worked. A vision of loveliness, as beautiful as the day I had left her. I said hello and I could see that she was shocked and surprised to see me. Anyway, she smiled back at me and I could tell that she still felt the same about me as I felt about her. I wanted take hold of her there and then. We started to see each other as often as possible but as I was working on the farm it was difficult except when I could get into town. One day she suggested I should come to The Haven when her husband was at work. I knew that this was a major step, but I loved her so much I could not resist her invitation. From then on we would meet regularly, but in secret.'

'So in the time before the accident you and Edna were having an affair,' said Madeleine.

'Yes, we were. In our own minds we rationalised it by saying that if the Army had not made such a blunder then we would be married anyway. The other thing was, although you may not think it a valid reason for her behaviour, she told me Stan used to beat her up. I saw her with a black eye once, but only once. After that he hit her where the bruises wouldn't show, but I saw them. She would cry in my arms with the pain.'

'I think we need a break, don't you?' said Ian, very conscious of how distressing this could be for Tina. 'Can I get anyone a drink? Tea, coffee or something stronger?'

'I'm driving,' said Kevin, 'so I'll have coffee, thanks.'

'Same for me,' said Tina, who was holding herself together very well.

'Make that three,' added John.

Ian and Madeleine went out into the kitchen to make the coffees.

'Got a bit tricky, hasn't it?' said Ian. 'What shall we do about Tina and Kevin? It looks as if the story isn't going to get any better from Stan's point of view. How do you think she'll take it? It's not very nice having your dad described as a wife-beater by some total stranger.'

'I'll have a word with her. Go back into the living room and ask her to join me in the kitchen. Tell her I want some help.'

Ian did as Madeleine had asked, and Tina came out into the kitchen.

'How can I help?' she asked

'It's more how I can help you. John Williams doesn't know that Stan Proctor is Eric Smith and therefore your dad. I don't know what he is going to say next, but I don't want it to upset you.'

'That's OK. I know what Dad was like. I know he had a temper, and I expect in those days it was different. Not right, but different. A man with a temper hit his wife when he was cross; it happened. Nowadays it's unacceptable so it happens less, although it still goes on. I hear people in our street sometimes, and I'm sure it's not just words but fists that are flying.'

Madeleine gave her a hug.

'I don't know how you manage to stay so calm,' said Madeleine.

'It's because I know I have someone who loves me to bits, and would never lay a finger on me. I have had problems in the past, with Brian, my ex, but not now. So I can take it.'

'Let's go back in, can you manage that tray for me. Thanks.'

Madeleine and Tina returned to the living room with the required drinks and biscuits. Madeleine stopped John continuing with his story while she explained that Stan Proctor and Eric Smith, Tina's father, were one and the same person. John looked at Tina apologetically.

'I'm so sorry, Tina, I didn't know. All I can say is what I saw, and what Edna told me. It was clear to me at the time that Stan used to knock her about a bit, but I feel dreadful telling this story now with you here.'

'Don't worry about that. As I was saying to Madeleine in the kitchen, I understand that, whilst unacceptable and wrong today, times were different then. It didn't make it right, I would not suggest that for a moment, but people's views of it were certainly different,' said Tina.

'Shall I carry on? I don't have to if you would prefer.'

'Please carry on, John.' Tina was feeling much more confident now. 'I want to know everything. He was my Dad after all, good and not-so-good.'

'Thank you, Tina. The next bit of the story is the most difficult bit for me,' admitted John.

He knew that this next piece of the story was what had stopped him all these years from talking about it to anyone.

'Stan was a bus driver,' continued John, 'and as such worked very regular hours. Edna always knew his timetable, so we would arrange our meetings accordingly. Tuesday afternoons were our favourite, because he was on the route out to Bridport those afternoons, and he was never back before six o'clock. We used to meet at two in the afternoon and spend an hour together. I could get away from the farm for an hour at that time, so it suited us fine.'

John looked across at Madeleine and Ian.

'This is where the cuckoo clock was important. Looking back I know that it sounds silly, but we would keep strictly to our timetable, guided by the cuckoo clock. Edna used to say that I was the cuckoo in her nest. I don't think that was ornithologically correct, but we were young lovers, so it didn't matter. We would come downstairs at three o'clock at the sound of the cuckoo, and we would say goodbye, so that I could get back to the farm at a reasonable hour.'

'That August Tuesday afternoon was no different. We lay in bed upstairs listening to the sound of the rain on the windows and the roof, and I was thankful that I was not out in the fields getting soaked. Just being with her in my arms was heaven for me, and it was with great reluctance that we got up when we heard the sound of the cuckoo. Having come downstairs I was holding Edna here, underneath the clock, when we heard him arrive. Then Stan Proctor came into the house calling, "hello darling".'

Because it was foul weather, but unbeknown to us, the bus services had been cancelled owing to the flooding, and the staff sent home.

Tina gasped, remembering what her father had said in one of his dementia-induced rages.

'And then he saw us. He flew across the room and as he did so he aimed a blow at me.'

John stopped and took deep breaths. This was what he was dreading, admitting to this behaviour. He gathered himself together and continued.

'I ducked and ran out of the door. The blow missed me and struck Edna on the side of the head. As she fell, she hit her head on the arm of the chair, and slumped onto the floor, stunned, her gown falling open. Stan was raging, cursing and shouting at her. He grabbed hold of her left hand and pulled at the ring on her finger. "You don't deserve it" he yelled.'

Tina put her hands up to her face as she again recognised the phrase.

'Her fingers must have been a little swollen, as he could not remove the ring, however much he pulled at it. I had run round to the side of the house and I was able to see what was happening through there.'

He pointed to the small window at the side of the room.

'I am so ashamed,' he said. 'I am so ashamed that I did nothing to help her. Stan was a big man, not very tall, but powerful. I was only small and I was scared of him. But I was transfixed by what he was doing. I couldn't stop him and yet I couldn't not watch. It was awful, and I have lived with it ever since. I am so ashamed I did nothing to help the woman I loved so much.'

'Stan couldn't get the ring off so he threw her hand back down, and stormed out. I was going to go back in, and then I saw him return with an axe from the barn. I could hardly watch. He lifted up her left hand, and held the ring finger across the edge of the table, chopping it off, taking the ring and throwing the finger on the floor. All this time Edna was groggy, but when he did that, she screamed and screamed. The storm was raging outside, so I was the only one who saw and heard what was happening, and I did nothing. Blood poured everywhere and he ran out of the door, slamming it behind him, shouting.'

'As soon as he had left I went back in and bandaged the hand as well as I could, but I could do nothing with the finger. I had learnt a little first aid in Korea which helped. Then I ran up the road and called an ambulance. I had to do it anonymously, because I shouldn't have been there. I waited until I heard the bell of the ambulance, then I left.'

John stopped, and held his head in his hands. He was totally drained.

'I never saw her again.'

There was silence in the room as John finished his story. Tina was in tears at the description of her father's behaviour and Kevin was trying to comfort her.

'Hitting her is one thing,' cried Tina through her tears unbelievingly, 'mutilating her is something else. Why didn't you go to the police or something?'

John Williams looked at her blankly.

'I don't know. I just don't know. Looking back now it seems the obvious thing to have done. But then...'

'Wouldn't the hospital have noticed bruising on her face and her missing finger when she went in?' asked Kevin, equally bewildered.

'I don't know how much notice they would have taken if Edna had said she had had an accident at home. These days hospitals are more suspicious of such explanations, but maybe then they would have taken her word for it.'

'A week later I had a letter from Edna,' said John, continuing his story, and he showed them the letter which had upset his mother so much. 'That ended our relationship, at least for the time being. I had to leave home, and she was pregnant, with Stan's child. I was not the father, as she says, but if I had continued seeing her then it would have appeared as if I were.'

'That explains the number and the Bible reference,' said Madeleine.

John looked at her, quizzically.

'When Eric died he left a piece of paper with a number written on it, 1510. When we, Tina and I that is, went to the solicitors to see about the package Eric had left with them, it had a biblical reference written on it. It was from the Book of Jeremiah in the Old Testament;

' *'I will punish you as your deeds deserve, declares the Lord.* ''

The number 1510 is a reference to the time, ten minutes past three in the afternoon. He is, in his own mind, justifying his treatment of Edna. Ten past three being the time he discovered what she was up to.'

''He must have done this later, after he had got away from the scene of the accident,' said Tina, 'do we know where he was before he came back?'

'No, I don't think we would ever discover that,' said Ian.

'After Edna came out of hospital, John, do you know what happened next?' asked Madeleine.

'I know that while in hospital she found out she was pregnant, and that pregnancy continued satisfactorily as far as I know. My parents had thrown me out, and I couldn't communicate with her any more.'

'So Edna sent you the cuckoo clock; why?'

'She sent the clock to Little Morton Farm, although she didn't know whether I was there. When she sent it to me, she wrote another letter. Unfortunately my mother recognised the writing on the parcel when it arrived and did nothing with it. By this time I was totally estranged from my parents, so I knew nothing about the second letter and the clock. It was about fifteen years later when my parents died. I think I said before that they died very close together. After Dad died there was no one who was willing and able to take on the farm, so I came back and did what was necessary to deal with their possessions. It was then that I discovered the parcel with the clock and the second letter.'

John picked up the letter from the bunch of papers he had brought with him.

'This is what she wrote to me when she sent the clock to me. You must remember that I had no knowledge of this for many years. The whole affair has blighted my life really. I know that I have been successful financially, but emotionally I have been a complete failure.'

He held his head in his hands again.

'How could I let him do that to her? I should have gone back in to her, and stood up to him. I just let him mutilate her in front of me. And after all that she wrote me this letter. I can't believe how she could still feel that way about me after I had let her down so badly.'

'I am sure,' said Madeleine, 'that she did not see it like that. Her love for you was strong enough to help her come to terms with what happened.'

'You must be right,' said John, 'read this.'

He handed the letter to Madeleine, who read it aloud.

4 October 1955

'My dearest John

I don't know whether you ever received my previous letter, but I do hope so. I understand from what people have said that you have left the area after a row with your parents. I am guessing they found out about us; was it from my letter? Anyway, as I don't have any other address I am sending this to the farm. Hopefully your parents will send it on to you if you have made it up.

Stan never came back. It was funny because his body was never found, so I don't know whether he escaped to a new life. Who knows? I had my baby on 2 April; he is lovely. I suppose all mums think their babies are the best, so I am no different. But all that is going to change. During my pregnancy there was a lot of talk about Stan not being the father, and that was why he had left home and not come back People stopped talking to me, and it became difficult in the shops when women stared at me and said nothing. People knew that you had left home, and that seemed to prove to them that you were the father of my baby. I lost my job at the bakery shop. Mr Young, the manager, said I was bad for business. Since I have had Paul, I have had trouble finding work. Who will employ a woman with a baby, especially if she has a reputation, however unjustified? Money has become very difficult, there is the family allowance which helps but...

I have decided, and it has been a very difficult decision, to put little Paul up for adoption. That way he will have a better life than I can possibly give him. I love him so much that I can see that this is the only way. I am going away, abroad probably, and I am going to try to make a new life. Then, perhaps, one day, I will be able to come back, and maybe he will understand when he grows up that what I have done is because of my love for him. I am going to change my name as well, for a completely fresh start. You know my Dad died when I was very little, and my Mum married again to a Keith Treacy. Shortly after I married Stan, Keith got a job in Canada on the railways, so he and Mum emigrated there. He was always very good to me, so in my new life I am going to be Miss Treacy.

I am also sending you the cuckoo clock. It is a reminder of me to you, and I will always remember you when I think of the clock. It was given to me on my sixteenth birthday by my Auntie, whose name was Mary Fraser. I used to admire it every time we went to visit her, and she promised it to me one day. It was such a nice surprise when she gave it to me. So, in memory of that, I am going to be Mary Treacy. When you do receive this, whenever it is, put the clock somewhere to remind you of me, and the special hours we spent together at The Haven.

John, I love you so much, but we cannot be together. I hope you have a happy life, and keep just a little space in your heart for someone who loved you more than she could ever say.

Edna

xxxxxx

The room fell silent as Madeleine finished reading the letter. Kevin put his arm around Tina and hugged her close. Ian was staring at the clock, wondering what John must be feeling. John, meanwhile, was distraught. His whole life was laid bare by these two letters, but he also felt a surge of relief, that at last he had been able to share this lifelong story with someone else. Madeleine was looking dumbfounded at the letter, as if she could not quite comprehend what she had just read.

John struggled to compose himself.

'So,' he said, 'that is who I wanted you to find; Paul. He would be in his late fifties now. I didn't want to tell you the whole story at the beginning, that's why I couldn't give you any further information.'

'I'm sorry, John,' said Madeleine, 'but we have got a little bit to add to the story.'

'About Paul?'

'Yes. Only a couple of weeks after this letter was written, Paul died from polio. Edna was the informant on the death certificate, so it doesn't look as if the adoption ever took place.'

'That's terrible. So she lost all she had,' said John.

'I am surprised she didn't tell you about Paul's death,' said Madeleine.

'Maybe she did,' said John, 'the clock arrived in a big parcel, you may have seen it in the barn, and the letter was inside the box. I don't think my parents would have thrown away a large parcel like that. But if there was a subsequent letter on its own, I would not be at all surprised if my mother burned it. Do you know what happened next? My solicitor told me that she had lived in France for many years and worked as a translator.'

'Mary went to France in late November,' said Madeleine, 'she travelled on a ship bound for South Africa and disembarked at Marseille. I would guess that she found work there. Could she speak French?'

'Not as far as I know. She was very bright and would have picked things up pretty quickly. The solicitor said that she had a slight stroke three years ago, and that was why she came back here.'

'I'm surprised she didn't get in touch,' said Ian.

'It was many, many years ago. Maybe she felt she couldn't risk it. Maybe she preferred her memories. I have often pictured us together, though. I have this recurring vision of us together in old age, with grandchildren and great-grandchildren, running rings round us.'

He could not stop the tears this time and he collapsed back in his chair.

'So Dad and Edna both changed their names and ended up living in Seatown. It's a miracle they didn't meet each other in that time,' said Tina. 'That would have been nice. I expect Dad would have been sorry for his behaviour all those years ago.'

Madeleine and Ian looked at each other, unsure that they were in agreement with Tina's rosy picture of a reconciliation between Stan and Edna.

'Who would like another drink?' asked Ian.

'Thanks,' said Tina, 'another cup of tea would go down a treat.'

'And me,' added Kevin.

Ian made his way into the kitchen to put the kettle on,

'What about you, John?' asked Madeleine.

John Williams was still silently sobbing, tears staining his face.

'Yes,' called Madeleine, 'make one for John as well.'

When Ian came through with the drinks John had recovered.

'Sorry about that,' John said, with the reticence expected from a man of his age and background.

'You will now understand, Madeleine,' he continued, 'why it was so necessary to have the right tenant here at The Haven. For many years I had the clock at my cottage in Steeple Morton, but when this house came up for sale I knew exactly what to do. I bought it immediately and set about improving it and furnishing it, so that, in my old man's imagination, I could put the clock here, and therefore put Edna here as well. I couldn't even bring myself to throw away the bits of furniture that were here when she was. In the intervening years most had been thrown away, but not all. If you have a look at the table in the barn you will see the cut in the top made by the axe. I know it's almost macabre to keep these things, but there we are.'

'When Mary/Edna came back from France she made a new will?' asked Madeleine.

'I don't know whether it was new or a replacement. But it was only a year ago. The solicitor said she asked about me but she didn't contact me, as I said. She had a small flat in town and a reasonable amount of savings, which she has left to me, but I don't feel I deserve it.'

'So she was still married to Dad when she died?' asked Tina. 'I wonder how he would have felt about that. When I used to visit him in the home he had these outbursts, I think I told you, Madeleine. I didn't know what they meant, but he was remembering that day, when he found Edna with you. It clearly stayed with him all his life.'

'It must have been a very powerful memory to come through like that,' said Kevin.

'If it hadn't been for Korea...' said John. 'I feel bad about Stan, but I had loved Edna since I was fourteen. And without the National Service...'

''And the blunder by the Army,' added Ian.

'You remember the photo I showed you of Edna leaning over the gate,' said John.

'Such a pretty girl,' said Kevin.

'Yes, she was. Well, I went to her funeral a few weeks ago and I sent some roses. I put a tag on them with the letters JTAJX. It seemed appropriate somehow. Je T'Aime John Kiss. She would have understood.'

They all sat in silence pondering on how lives can be torn apart by random events over which one has little or no control. Tina stood up, hesitantly.

'I'm sorry but we will have to go. Kevin has an early start tomorrow. Thank you Madeleine, Ian, and John, of course. It's a very sad tale all round. Is there anything we can do to help?'

'There is one thing,' said John, 'I need to go to see my solicitors, Hughes and Lewis, tomorrow morning.

Would you be able to come with me? There is something which might affect you, and I think it would be a good idea if you were there.'

'Hughes and Lewis? That's where Dad left his envelope with that Bible reference on. How odd.'

She looked at Kevin for approval and he nodded.

'I won't be able to come,' he said, 'but you go. Maybe Madeleine could go with you. Would that be OK John?'

'Yes. I'll call Jeremiah first thing; then I'll pick you up about eleven.'

Tina agreed and said she would see him the following day. As they left John stood up as well.

'Thank you Madeleine. It has been a great relief, although emotionally very hard as well. I'll see you in the morning, about half past ten?'

John, Tina and Kevin left, leaving Ian and Madeleine to think about the evening's developments. They collapsed into the armchairs and looked at each other, trying to take in everything that they had learned, and trying to understand why it all happened as it did.

'How romantic and how sad, all at the same time,' said Madeleine. 'John and Edna were clearly very much in love. But poor old Stan. I know he did some dreadful things, and I am not excusing what he did, but finding his pretty wife in another man's arms can't have been easy. He was a good man to his second wife, though, and she treated him badly. Funny old world. I thought Tina was remarkable; being able to take all that in about her father without recriminations. I think that Kevin is the key there; she is very secure with him. On a different tack, though, there is something that cropped up tonight which was strange; to do with the clock.'

'What was that?' asked Ian, enjoying this late evening with Madeleine.

'John said that Edna told him that she was given the cuckoo clock by her aunt on her sixteenth birthday.'

'So?'

'She said her aunt's name was Mary Fraser. My grandmother's name was Mary Fraser, and my mum said that she used to have a cuckoo clock. I don't know what happened to that clock. Do you think that Edna's aunt and my granny are one and the same person? And that that cuckoo clock up there used to belong in my family?'

'There's one way to find out,' said Ian, 'employ someone to trace your family tree, there's an advert in the parish magazine. You ought to ring her up,' he added, laughing, 'I've got to go. I'll see you on Sunday.'

Ian pecked her on the cheek as he walked out.

Chapter Thirty Two

John Williams collected Madeleine promptly the next morning for their visit to Hughes and Lewis, and then took a detour to the other side of town to collect Tina. Tina settled back in the plush seats of John's Jaguar; she had never been in a car this luxurious before. When they had arrived home the previous evening, both Tina and Kevin had been overwhelmed by the revelations about Edna and Stan. Tina was torn between her natural affection for her father and her revulsion at his treatment of his wife. She had difficulty reconciling this with the man she knew and loved; the man who, although she knew had had a temper, had never laid a finger on her own mother.

It was all a long time ago, Kevin said, and times were different. Tina knew this and said so herself, but hearing the graphic details made it worse. Stan's actions were unacceptable in any era, she thought. She went on to remember what she had felt about Brian, her husband, when she discovered his string of affairs. Given different circumstances, who knows what might she have done to him?

That morning, after Kevin had left for work, these thoughts had been swirling through Tina's mind. She thought of nothing else as the car took her across town and pulled up outside the solicitors. It stopped as silently as it had been travelling. John got out and opened the doors for her and Madeleine. Walking into the office, Tina caught sight of George Hastings and smiled. George looked back vacantly, not recognising the two women.

'Come in, John, good to see you,' said Jeremiah as the three of them were shown into his office. 'And you must be Mrs Porter and Ms Jenkins. Do sit down. I have asked for coffee and tea to be brought up.'

Tina looked around the room; it was like something out of a film; the walls lined with leather books, the heavy furniture and grand table and chairs. It was not like any office she had been in before, she thought, and completely unlike the rest of the offices, which were modern and clean-cut.

Jeremiah sat behind his polished mahogany desk, and leaned back, expectantly.

'Now what is all this about, John? Have you come to tell me those secrets you weren't telling me before?'

He chuckled as he saw John Williams shift uncomfortably in his chair. Before he could answer there was a knock on the door and a severely dressed woman came in carrying the coffee on a tray.

'I'll be back with the tea in a moment, Mr Lewis,' she said.

'Thank you, Miss Partington, on the table there will be fine.'

The stern Miss Partington returned shortly with the tea tray. Nothing more was said between her and Mr Lewis.

'A formidable woman,' said Jeremiah, 'but I couldn't do without her. What she doesn't know about this firm would go on a stamp.'

Tina looked worried.

'Don't worry, my dear,' said Jeremiah to her, 'I don't think the Gestapo could make her reveal anything. Now, what's it all about?'

John and Madeleine together told him the tale of Stan, Edna and John. Madeleine explained how she had uncovered details about the Haven Horror incident and its repercussions, and how she had identified Eric Smith as being the same man as Stan Proctor. She also filled him in with the details of the cuckoo clock.

'I see why you were reticent,' said Jeremiah, looking at John, 'but I have something here which may help you, Ms Jenkins.'

He took out of a folder on his desk the envelope with the Bible text and the number on the outside. The envelope had been opened, and he pulled out a document which he opened on the desk.

'As you suspected,' he said, 'this is a deed poll, a change of name document, evidencing the change of name from Stanley Proctor to Eric Smith. What did surprise me was that this document was executed in 1954, on 31

August. It was drawn up by a firm of solicitors in Exeter, Field and Stubbings. I have made enquiries and this firm closed down in 1959. I would guess that Mr Proctor, or Mr Smith as he was by then, lodged the document with them, and it was returned to him when the firm closed down. As we did not draw up the document it is unusual that it has been deposited with us. Normally we would not take in documents from clients for storage. He may, of course, have come to us on another matter and left it with us then.'

'That means Dad was in Exeter in 1959?'

'Not necessarily. It just means that the solicitors there knew where to contact him. From what you have said, you know he didn't return to Seatown until 1959/60, so it's most likely that he was there,' said Jeremiah.

'I would guess,' said Madeleine, 'that when he escaped from the accident on that day, he was able to get to Exeter, maybe by hitching, and then he stayed there until he learned of his sister's illness.'

'There is something else,' said Jeremiah.

He tipped the envelope upside down and a ring slid out onto the desk.

'Edna's wedding ring,' gasped John. 'He kept it all these years. That's what he said she didn't deserve.'

'As it was hers, it is yours now,' Jeremiah said, 'along with her other belongings and personal effects.'

'I can't take it,' said John, 'it was Stan's, Tina should have it.'

'Not legally.' said Jeremiah. 'It was Edna's, now it's yours.'

'Well, just keep it for the time being. Anyway I've been thinking,' said John, 'and this is the reason we have come today. As Stan didn't die in the accident he was still married to Edna. Edna died shortly before Stan, so if she had not made a will, Stan would have got everything. Is that right?'

'Yes,' said Jeremiah, cautiously.

'So if Edna had known about Stan still being alive, she might have not made me the beneficiary.'

'We can't second-guess such things, John. As I understand it, Stan mutilated her hand, and then left her. Why would she leave him anything after that?'

'As you said Jeremiah, we can't second-guess her. However we do know that she was considerably younger than Stan, and by the time she made the will it would not be unreasonable for her to assume he was dead. Is it possible for me to reject the inheritance, and ask you to give it to Tina instead? She is Stan's only living relative.'

Tina stared at John, disbelievingly.

'John,' said Jeremiah, 'do you mean that you don't want what Mary has left you?'

'I don't deserve it after how I deserted her. I have the clock; that is enough for me. Give it to Tina.'

'I'm sorry, John. That's not possible. It is not for me to effectively alter Mary's will like that. There is an alternative, though. What you can do is to reject the legacy, and that would have the same result.'

'How would that work?' asked John.

'As you are the sole beneficiary, and there is no one else to benefit under the will, the estate would have to be dealt with under the laws of intestacy.'

'What does that mean?' asked Madeleine.

'It would be the same as if Mary had not made a will, except that as her executor it is my duty to distribute the estate properly.'

'But who gets the estate under these laws?' pressed Madeleine.

'The laws of intestacy set out clearly the beneficiaries where no will has been made...'

'Cut to the chase Jeremiah, for goodness sake,' interrupted John, 'Where does the estate go?'

'As she was still married to Stan at the time of her death, he would be her sole beneficiary,' said Jeremiah, 'and on his death it would pass under his will.'

'He left everything to me,' said Tina.

'In that case, Mary's estate would come to you. Did your father make a will?'

'Yes,' replied Tina, 'you are dealing with it.'

Jeremiah turned back to John.

'Are you certain that you want to reject this legacy? If so, I will have the appropriate form drawn up for you to sign. Once you have signed it you will not be able to change your mind. Maybe it would be better for you to think it over.'

'I am certain,' said John, 'draw up the form and I will sign it. I don't want to think about it any more. I have decided.'

Jeremiah pressed a button on his desk and Miss Partington came in. Jeremiah had a few words with her before she left without speaking.

'The form will be ready for you to sign later today or tomorrow, whichever suits you best.'

Tina sat, overwhelmed by what was going on.

'So I get Edna's money? How much is that? Oh dear, I'm not sure; how would Edna feel about Stan's daughter getting her money?'

'About £100,000, or a bit more. There was a flat in town and there were some savings. The flat has been sold for £95000, but there will be some expenses to pay out of that,' said Jeremiah, 'as far as Edna is concerned she...'

'Don't worry about Edna,' interrupted Madeleine. 'I am sure that she would be pleased that her money was going to someone who will benefit greatly from it. You must tell Kevin.'

'Yes, of course,' said Tina, still coming to grips with inheriting over £100,000 from someone she never knew. 'Yes.'

John stood to leave and shook Jeremiah's hand.

'I'll leave you to sort it all out. I'll drop in tomorrow to sign the form. Look after Tina for me; she'll need your guidance.'

'Yes, I will,' said Jeremiah, 'goodbye; goodbye Mrs Porter and Ms Jenkins. I'll be in touch with you, Ms Jenkins.'

As they left John Williams felt a load lifted from him. He still had the beautiful memories of Edna, but without the guilt that had dogged him all his life. The cuckoo clock would stay at The Haven, in Madeleine's good care. He had in mind offering her a longer tenancy than the original six months. He hoped she would agree to that, but he decided it would be better speak to her another time about that.

Tina was beginning to understand what difference her inheritance would make to her and Kevin, not forgetting Jimmy. As she left she rang him to bring tell him her news, but he was unavailable and she left him a message. She was very thrilled that she had such good news for him when his job was under threat.

Madeleine was looking forward to bringing Ian up to date with developments. She rang him as soon as she arrived home, and he said he would call in later. She could hardly wait, but while she was doing so, she checked some family research of her own. Ian arrived in the late afternoon and Madeleine told him the whole story. He was pleased that Tina was going to benefit from the whole saga; she deserved it, he thought.

'And I have some other news,' Madeleine said. 'This afternoon I was re-checking my own family history. My great-grandparents were Alexander Wood and Susan Luce, and they had two children, Mary in 1902 and Emily seven years later, in 1909. Mary Wood married Michael Fraser in 1925 and they are my grandparents on my mother's side. Emily Wood married William Fox in 1931 and they had a daughter, Edna. William Fox died in 1933 and Emily married again to a Keith Treacy in 1934. Edna said in her letter to John that her aunt, Mary Fraser, gave her the cuckoo clock on her sixteenth birthday. That was in 1948, when my mother was in her early twenties. We had very little to do with that side of the family. From my own research I knew that my grandmother had a sister Emily, but I did not know her family and certainly did not know where they lived. It seems as if my great-aunt Emily was Edna's mother.'

'I think, therefore,' she said, pointing upwards, 'that is the same clock that my mother said my granny had, but she, Mum, didn't know what had happened to it.'

Ian laughed.

'So are you going to tell John the clock's yours after all then?'

Madeleine was unsure whether to tell John Williams of her family connection with the clock. It had been given to Edna many years ago, and she did not wish to appear to be making any claim on it, but she thought he might be fascinated to learn that it had found a very appropriate custodian. When Fiona, Tim and Joseph came to visit the following week, though, she did tell them. Joseph was lying contentedly in his crib in the living room when the clock cuckooed, and he gurgled happily at the noise.

'Sorry, Tim,' laughed Madeleine, 'I told you that your offspring would like Auntie Madeleine's clock. You'll just have to put up with it.'

'OK, I will, 'said Tim, 'but you need to tell us the full story.'

Madeleine settled back in the armchair.

'There's a lot to tell; so are you sitting comfortably? Then I'll begin.'

Joseph dozed happily, while doting adults listened to the tale of his great-grandmother's clock.

22500944R00158

Printed in Great Britain
by Amazon